The
Cupcake
Cottage

THE CUPCAKE COTTAGE

A HOCKEY SWEETHEART NOVEL

JEAN ORAM

The Cupcake Cottage
by Jean Oram
Copyright © 2022 Jean Oram
All rights reserved.
First Edition

Printed in the United States of America unless otherwise stated on the last page of this book. Published by Oram Productions Alberta, Canada.

COMPLETE LIBRARY OF CONGRESS CATALOGING-IN-PUBLICATION DATA AVAILABLE ONLINE
Oram, Jean.
The Cupcake Cottage / Jean Oram.—1st. ed.
ISBN: 978-1-989359-88-4, 978-1-989359-94-5
Ebook ISBN: 978-1-989359-70-9
Large Print: 978-1-989359-89-1

First Oram Productions Edition: May 2022

Cover design by Jean Oram

There was nothing like a herd of hunky, strong athletic men fighting over a frozen black puck. Or an oblong football. Or riding on the back of an angry bronco.
It didn't matter the sport, Daisy-Mae had a thing for jocks.

This book goes out to readers who feel the same way Daisy-Mae does.

ACKNOWLEDGMENTS

A special thank you goes to Nate who not only named several characters in this new series, but also wrote me a kitten scene when I told him I'd do his math for him. (I was joking.) And yet I've never seen a nine-year-old write over two-hundred words so quickly.

Thank you goes to my readers who waited over a year for this book to be ready.

Absolutely no thank-yous go to the character Daisy-Mae who had me delete over half of her book. Seriously!

Thanks to my editor, my error team and my Jeansters. Hugs and love!

FOREWORD

About time this Canadian wrote a hockey romance, eh?

XO,
Jean Oram
(Writing away in a Canadian spring snowstorm)
April, 2022

CHAPTER 1

*D*aisy-Mae Ray made her way down the arena's concrete steps, guiding the San Antonio Dragons' mascot. She'd taken the job as a mascot handler in the NHL for two reasons. Debt and debt.

Well, the second reason was actually so she could be closer to the team captain, Maverick Blades. But as a woman who'd officially hit her thirties, it was entirely too humiliating to admit that. Especially when her longtime acquaintance likely had no clue how badly she was crushing on him.

The human-sized plush dragon beside Daisy-Mae suddenly plummeted downward, and Violet squeaked from inside the giant head, her short arms flailing.

"Sorry!" Daisy-Mae scrambled to right her friend before she slipped down another step and twisted an ankle.

"Don't let me die a humiliating death!" Violet adjusted the dragon head, which had turned sideways.

Daisy-Mae guided her down a few more steps to a small landing overlooking center ice. "Sorry."

"Come on! We're the Dragon Babes! A new life outside of Sweetheart Creek full of mani-pedis, parties, and lunching out with players' wives. Hot jocks and

1

fun! We can't be the babes if you let me fall and die."
She giggled, the sound muffled by the giant head she
was wearing but coming through Daisy-Mae's earpiece
loud and clear. "Although I'm pretty sure I'd bounce in
this thing." She patted the dragon's stuffed belly.

"Don't try it," Daisy-Mae warned her.

"Are we on the landing?"

"Yes. Do you want to practice a few moves?"

Violet waved to the empty arena where the Zamboni was driving in circles, resurfacing the ice. She held
her head, covered her eyes with her giant costume
hands, and turned away from the ice as though something bad had happened. Then she waggled her short
dragon tail toward the rink and wiggled her hands near
her ears like she was egging on an opponent.

Daisy-Mae laughed. "Who *are* you in there, Dezzie
Dragon?" Her friend might be part wallflower in real
life, but she came alive in the costume. She'd thought
Violet was kidding when she said she was trying out
for this position. Daisy-Mae had flippantly retorted
that if Violet got the job, she'd apply to be her handler.

And now here she was.

Honestly, it was probably one of her better life
choices. Even though the job was part-time and over an
hour's drive from her home in Sweetheart Creek, she
was paid enough that she could close up several of her
at-home businesses. Not that they brought in much,
but still—their income had helped her eke out a living.
Maybe her mom was right and former beauty queens
weren't cut out for business.

"You liked the tail wag?" Violet asked, doing it again.

"It was good. Very expressive. Want to go all the
way down to the ice?"

Dezzie's giant head wobbled.

"Was that a yes? If so, put more of your torso into it."

Violet tried again and Dezzie's whole body swayed forward dangerously. Afraid she was going to topple, Daisy-Mae grabbed her in a bear hug.

"What are you doing?" Violet asked.

"It looked like you were falling."

"Well, you can hug me any time, because with Owen going back to baseball..." She let out a raspberry sound from inside her costume.

Violet had only just been getting her feet back under her romantically after being dumped at the altar a few years ago. She'd been closing in on Owen Lancaster, the two flirting like mad, when he suddenly had a big fight with his dad about the family ranch, then up and rejoined major league baseball, moving thousands of miles away.

If Daisy-Mae thought she had bad dating luck, Violet's was even worse.

The Zamboni finished polishing the oval rink and exited the ice via its gate, leaving a shiny trail behind it like an oversized snail.

"What's that sound?" Violet asked.

"The Zamboni doors are closing."

Dezzie did a dance. "Yippee! Send out the hotties!"

"Violet!" Daisy-Mae laughed, her cheeks heating with embarrassment.

"I'm marrying a Dragon this season."

"Me, too." Daisy-Mae just wished she didn't sound so wistful.

"You're going to have them fighting over you. Save at least one for me, okay?" Violet gripped her head, maneuvering the costume, presumably so she could spy through the eyeholes a bit better. "Do you see any hotties yet?"

"Nope. Not yet." She could hear some deep voices, but so far nobody had appeared.

3

"Betcha five bucks you have two Dragon proposals by December."

"I wish." Daisy-Mae had come from a long line of women who got married straight out of high school, but she'd never once been proposed to. At least not by anyone who wasn't falling down drunk or joking.

Daisy-Mae directed Violet along a walkway that ran parallel with the ice before taking several more steps down. She shivered, rethinking her fitted checked blouse, which was tied at her navel. It was cold in the arena despite San Antonio's early October temperatures.

Hockey players hit the ice, their blades shaving the frozen surface, and Daisy-Mae forgot her chill. Their deep voices filled the air, and she shivered again, but now for a new reason. There was nothing like a herd of hunky, strong, athletic men fighting over a frozen black puck. Or an oblong football. Or riding on the back of an angry bronco.

It didn't matter the sport. Daisy-Mae had a thing for jocks.

Violet and Daisy-Mae made it down to ice level where the rink's boards and Plexiglass protected them from errant pucks, giving them a thrilling close-up of the players. The team was skating around the perimeter to warm their muscles, zipping past the women.

Daisy-Mae waved to a few of the men as they glided past. A couple of rookies waved back, unable to block out the attention from the empty stands during today's closed practice. Daisy-Mae scanned the men, searching for their captain, Maverick Blades. She had a secret, teensy, growing fantasy where he'd spot her in the stands and his pale blue eyes would lock on hers. A private moment would pass between them, and she'd feel as though he truly saw her amid the hubbub as the

4

game roared on. Weeks later he'd casually ask her out for dinner, then an awards banquet where he would get another plaque or golden hockey stick or whatever players won. He'd break his don't-date-them-twice rule, and they'd become inseparable. Soon after, he would propose to her on center ice after winning a cup. Everyone would be celebrating, but he'd ignore it all, take off his helmet and get down on one knee. His gorgeous eyes with those ridiculous dark lashes would meet hers and he'd say—

"I can't see!"

"What?"

"I can't see!" Violet sounded like a toddler about to have a meltdown.

Daisy-Mae quickly adjusted Violet's head, shifting it back into place. "Better?"

Violet waved at the passing men, continuing through the routine she'd learned during her training. "You'd think the ice would melt these men are so hot."

Daisy-Mae laughed as she scanned the players. She finally spotted Maverick, her heart skipping faster. She'd almost won spending Valentine's Day with him last February. That had been a disappointing miss. Not that she'd admit it to anyone. Crushing after a man that was so obviously out of her league? She was probably too old for that, too.

One of the players waved at them each time he passed. Daisy-Mae smiled and waggled her red-tipped fingers. You never knew where your next Mr. Right might be hiding. And the man in the black helmet, practice jersey, and white hockey socks could be the one. He was fast, cute, and likely earned more in a month than Daisy-Mae did in a decade.

"Was that Leo?" Violet asked.

"I don't know."

"He used to be a bull rider."

5

"Are you crushing on him?"

"Nah, he's just a friend."

How had she even had the time to befriend players already?

Possibly-Leo came around again as Violet practiced some of her dance moves, bumping into Daisy-Mae who laughed as she nearly fell into one of the seats.

On the next pass, Maverick closed in behind him.

The player slowed slightly, calling out a "Hello, ladies!" Maverick, his stick held in both hands, used it to gently push the man's back. Daisy-Mae heard Maverick's gruff voice telling the man to focus.

Violet turned to Daisy-Mae. "Was that Maverick? What did he say?"

"Focus."

"I want to know what he said," she said in a pouty voice.

"That is what he said. He told him to focus."

"Told you! Proposals by Christmas!" Violet said triumphantly. "But seriously? They were nuts putting Maverick front and center as captain after all that bad press."

"He has the most experience, is the best defender in the division, made all-star when he was playing for—"

"Do you know those kinds of facts about everyone on the team or just your ex's BFF?"

"*And* he can bring a team together," Daisy-Mae said, her heart hammering. "He got traded because the Dragons need him."

And no, she didn't know any stats about the other Dragons.

"He didn't get traded. He got the boot because of the Lafayette mess. They had to get rid of him even though he's strong."

Daisy-Mae clamped her mouth shut. There was no way the rumors about Maverick and the Blur owner's wife were even close to true. Women falling all over Mav? Yeah, that was one hundred percent legit. But him getting involved with a married woman? No way. His mama had raised him right, and he had Texas honor ground into his soul.

Some might argue that money and fame could corrupt anyone, but she knew it couldn't change Maverick. That would be as easy as changing the direction of the sunset. It just wasn't going to happen.

"I heard they didn't have a choice whether to accept him," Violet continued. "Forced trade."

"You know, the team's publicists really need to do their job."

"Don't you dare fall for him," Violet chirped. "That man needs some serious work, and he'll break your heart. He hasn't been seen with the same woman twice —other than what's-her-face-married-chick and that introvert from years ago. He's the kind of man your mom warns you about."

"My mom warns me about *all* men who don't propose after three dates. And Lafayette was bad news right from the start. The Blur's owner is as sketchy as..." She shuddered, thinking of the vibes Adwin Kendrik gave off. He got wins and was celebrated in the world of the NHL like he was some sort of god, but just looking at photos of him stirred up that gut feeling. "Anyway, none of that matters because I'm not Mav's type."

She wasn't even close to a college-educated, sophisticated career babe.

Violet snorted. "You're every man's type. And Maverick is every woman's type—all hot and tall and unattainable. Total fantasy. I bet he accounts for at least half of any ticket sales made to women."

Daisy-Mae smiled. Yeah, she'd buy a ticket to watch him skate across the ice. Right now he was practically floating along, making skating look like the most natural thing. And he was tough during games too, sending grown men into the boards as though they were unsuspecting pedestrians taken out by a Mack truck. Nothing got between him and the puck.

As Maverick made his way around the rink again, he took his eyes off the man in front of him long enough to give Daisy-Mae a subtle head nod and maintain a beat of eye contact that made her stomach flip. Then he was gone.

She spun, watching him race around the curve, her hands pressed against the cold Plexiglass.

That had felt exactly like it did in her best fantasies.

Which meant trouble.

Trouble for her heart, as it was in the process of informing her that it was locked and loaded for one man, and one man only—Maverick Blades.

She needed to get ahold of herself. He was so far out of her league she could barely even *see* his league. She took a steadying breath and stepped away from the glass, her eyes still locked on his form. The man's strength and agility were clear as he performed flawless crossovers, his confidence solid in the thin metal blades beneath him. Sexy. So very sexy.

"I can't see much from in here, but I saw *that*," Violet murmured, her tone amused. "You're smitten with Mr. Bad Boy."

Daisy-Mae cleared her throat and tried to school her expression, certain she was close to drooling. But she couldn't seem to shake the overpowering thought that kept running through her mind: she needed to fix Number 53's reputation, and then maybe, just maybe, make him hers.

MAVERICK BLADES COASTED to the gate to exit the rink. He gave his helmet's chin strap a sharp yank, releasing the snap before slipping the rig from his head. His hair was soaked with sweat, each passing year requiring more effort to prove himself on the ice with the latest batch of fully energized rookies. He remembered that unstoppable feeling of youth. He didn't recall being as cocky as some of them, although he was pretty certain he had been.

He led the line of players to the locker room, thinking about today's practice and how soothing the frigid ice bath would feel on his screaming muscles. Thirty-one years of age wasn't young in the NHL. Still, he was holding on to his title as the top defender in the division.

Louis Bellmore, the team's head coach as well as a good friend, was waiting near the locker room door.

"Good practice out there, team. Don't forget to pick up a copy of your finalized diet plan." Louis raised his voice to ensure the line of tired players heard him. "Athena left copies by the door—be sure to take your own. They are labeled."

There was a round of "You got it, coach."

Before Maverick could enter the locker room, Louis jerked his chin toward his right shoulder, indicating Maverick should join him. The team filtered past as he stepped aside.

"What did you do now, Blades? Date a woman more than once?" one of the rookies chirped.

"Yup," he teased back. "Getting soft in my old age."

"You said it. Not us," Leo, Maverick's favorite rookie, said with a loud laugh. The kid, already in his late twenties but new to the NHL, had so much talent that Maverick wished hazing was still allowed, just so he could ensure the rookie remembered there was a pecking order. And that he wasn't at the top of it. Not yet, anyway.

"One day you'll grow a personality, Socks," he called after Leo. "Looking forward to that day."

"I hate that nickname," he called back. "I go by Blaze, thank you."

"Blaze is what a fifteen-year-old calls her barrel-racing horse."

"You lose your socks before our first exhibition game, the nickname sticks," Landon, the second oldest player on the ice, chimed in.

"I swear someone stole them from my locker."

Landon gave Maverick a commiserating pat on the back as he hobbled past in his goalie gear. "Keep on fighting for us old guys."

"Fight the Alzheimer's and arthritis, old man!" Leo cackled.

Maverick smirked, knowing his life could be a lot harder than a few teasing jabs. Despite his humiliating mid-season trade last year, and the swirling rumors that had come with him, the team had mostly accepted him as their captain.

Louis and Maverick moved down the hallway for more privacy.

"You were looking good out there," Louis stated.

Maverick ran a hand through his hair, mussing up the damp locks out of habit from his times going on camera immediately after a game. "Thanks."

"Think we'll have a good season?"

"Leo is green but learned a lot during his short time in the minors. More than most. And he's eager to pick up what he doesn't know. He'll win some cups during his career."

"He was a decent pick." Louis was quiet for a beat. "So were you."

"I know there was no choice." Not this time.

"I came out on top."

That was a generous statement coming from a man coaching an expansion team. As they were new to the league, the owner was working hard to gather players and investors, and having to take on a player with bad press and a high salary wasn't a position he'd ever want to be in. The Dragons needed some wins and some fans, and Maverick feared he'd be unable to deliver either.

Louis grew quiet, arms crossed as he watched Maverick from under the brim of his Dragons ball cap. "I made you captain because you're good with the guys and you keep the team focused."

Focused. He nearly scoffed. He'd practically tripped over his own stick when he spotted Daisy-Mae in the stands earlier. His buddy Myles Wylder's ex-girlfriend. Little Miss Cutoffs with legs that went clear to her ears, a generous smile, and a kind and gentle heart that made him want to pull her into his arms every time he saw her. Seeing as she was Off Limits thanks to the stupidest honor system known to man—the Bro Code—he did what he could to avoid her.

That was when he wasn't trying to accidentally-on-purpose bump into her somewhere just to feel the force of that mega-watt smile. He was a sucker for her casual insights and the way they made him believe he'd been seen by someone who didn't want something from him.

If she was truly the mascot handler, like she'd appeared to be today, the team would never win a home game. The woman could give Miss America a run for her money, and she was probably now the not-so-secret weakness of at least ninety percent of his teammates. Ninety-five, if he included himself. He only hoped that visiting teams would face the same lack of immunity to her focus-breaking charms and miss as many passes as the Dragons had today.

"I need your head in the game and in practices," Louis said, his tone firm and slightly reprimanding.

"Yes, Coach." He lowered his gaze, embarrassed by how distracted he'd been.

Louis's chest expanded as he held in a breath. From experience, Maverick knew he likely had about ten thousand things to say and was deciding where to start. They were all probably things Maverick didn't want to hear.

He shifted in his skates and waited.

"This team is an opportunity for both of us to end our careers on a high note. Problem is, the press is still looking to skewer you."

And that would impact the team. Nobody wanted to watch a home-wrecker—which the press seemed to think he was—earn big bucks on the ice.

Louis sighed when Maverick remained quiet. He'd known Louis for a long time, having skated under him during his rookie year in the NHL back in Toronto. The man knew him, his mom, and what he stood for. He was like family, and he wouldn't push something that shouldn't be pushed, but he was looking like a man debating pushing something. Something important.

"Miranda wants you to talk to PR."

It must be worse than he thought if the team's owner wanted him to go to the publicity team. Did that mean he was hurting ticket sales, sponsorship opportunities, and investor confidence, and that he needed to do something sweet in public such as save some puppies from burning buildings? Because if it was as bad as he feared, then by association alone, he was impacting the rookies and their ability to strike deals as well.

That was pretty uncool.

All because he'd stepped in to help someone.

"Talk about what?" he asked, hoping for a hint so he didn't go into the meeting blind.

"Just to work on your image and such. You up for that?"

"Yes, sir."

The so-called twins were supposed to be an amazing public relations duo from New York, but they didn't know Texas, and they didn't know the NHL. They'd have him wearing pink and knitting baby booties to rebuild his reputation if given the chance. Not command him to immediately rescue some golden retriever puppies.

However, if it took the worried tone out of his mother's voice whenever she called after hearing yet another fabricated news story about him, he'd do it.

"Whatever it takes," Maverick said, hoping he wouldn't regret his words.

"Are you willing to share your side of the story from Lafayette?"

"You know I can't. Not without hurting someone."

"Reanna seems okay with you suffering damage."

Yeah, she did. But that was understandable, as it was dangerous for her to expose her side of the story: the truth.

"I made a promise."

"How's your mother handling all of this?"

"Leave her out of this," Maverick warned. He hated how performing a series of good deeds was impacting his mom's ability to hold her head up high in Sweetheart Creek. He often lay awake at night, trying to rebuild the past or find a new way through the mess with Reanna that didn't lead to his negative new image. So far, he hadn't found one. Not one that would have also kept Reanna safe.

The two of them were barely even friends. That was the tough part.

Louis sighed and lifted his hands to show he was backing off. "Fine. Have a shower and go talk to the twins. They'll be waiting for you."

"I'll do whatever it takes, Lou. I promise you that. I'll even wear pink booties if it helps." Louis gave him a pained look of confusion. "I'll do anything—unless it involves me getting married or something." He smiled to show he was joking and trying to lift the heavy mood.

Louis didn't laugh.

Maverick stared at Louis, waiting for the man's somber expression to crack.

"Lou...man... I was joking. You know the only commitment I have time for is hockey." He'd learned that four years ago with Janie. Maintaining a relationship was nearly impossible when he was deep into a season. Coach had to be pulling his leg with that meaningful look of his. "Nobody'll believe I'm ready for that kind of business. I don't even have a girlfriend."

"Then you'd better come up with a stronger idea for mending your image, because according to what I've heard from the twins, it's that or taking on a princess mascot."

CHAPTER 2

"I still can't believe you didn't get fired for sass-talking the publicity team. You must have someone helping you on the inside."

Daisy-Mae turned toward the deep voice, knowing without looking that it was Maverick, and that his words were directed at her and that he was referencing the outburst she'd had at work almost two weeks ago.

"Thanks for the vote of confidence!" she said.

He joined her at the white fence overlooking the pastures that ran into the Texas hills beyond the Wylder's backyard. Behind them and across the lawn, strings of lights lit up the stone patio at the back of the sprawling ranch house as dusk slowly settled in. The yard was filled with what seemed like half of Sweetheart Creek, here to celebrate Karen and Myles's engagement. Her friend and her ex-boyfriend. She was happy for them both but couldn't help wondering when Cupid was going to get around to finding someone for her, too.

Although these days Cupid would need pretty fast wings to catch up with her. Life had become a blur—and even more so since she'd stood up for Maverick in front of the PR team.

"Hey, it's not every day a small-town bumpkin gives an NHL publicity team from New York what for—and lives to tell about it." Maverick was all grins and as handsome as ever in his suit jacket, jeans, and cowboy boots.

"Maybe I'm more than meets the eye." She gave him a playful jab in the ribs while batting her lashes. Truthfully, she was still embarrassed by the outburst. The PR team had wanted to talk strategy about her wardrobe as Dezzie's handler. She'd been dressing like a puck bunny with a Dragons jersey tied at the waist, tight jeans, boots, and a Dragons cowboy hat at the home games, but they'd decided they wanted a princess. As in, a full-out princess to fulfill the dragon fairy-tale theme—and they were going to spread that theme throughout the entire arena.

Seriously? NHLers with a princess mascot? Were they writing the book on emasculation? As if the Dragons didn't already have enough stacked against them as the worst-ranked, newest team in the league.

So, with little more than a thought beyond how embarrassing it would be for a man like Maverick, she'd opened her big mouth and told them exactly how she felt they should do their jobs. Then, once her brain had caught up with her, she'd excused herself, certain she was fired—only a few days into her new job.

"That's why I told Miranda to promote you to the ticket holder experience manager."

"Wait. That was you?" The promotion that had resulted from her rant had stunned her. But to know that Maverick had helped orchestrate it? That made her weak in the knees. Nobody had ever done something so incredibly sweet for her before. Or thrown her so far out of her skill set. She literally had no credentials and was in charge of hundreds of thousands of dollars' worth of merchandising and events for fans.

She had ideas, sure. They were so obvious to her—like team-sponsored tailgate parties with lots of free swag before games—but everyone was grabbing at them like they were pure gold. She was certain they'd soon discover she was just some high-school graduate, country bumpkin who didn't really belong there.

"Anyone who shoots down a princess theme earns my loyalty," Maverick said. "Trust me."

His look suggested that the PR team had tried to get him on board with the princess-and-the-dragon theme as well.

"Didn't I earn your loyalty years ago?" She gave him a sassy look, hands on her hips.

"Nope."

"Not even that time I pretended to be your girlfriend so that gal would take a hint during World Juniors and stop throwing her bra at you whenever you left the ice?"

He laughed, shaking his head. "That was so embarrassing."

"Funny though." He'd turned such an endearing shade of red each time. And here, almost fifteen years later, he was still running through that same color spectrum just talking about it.

"Do you know how mad Myles got at me because I borrowed you like that?"

"I don't think he expected you to hold my hand."

"At least I didn't sneak a kiss."

His gaze traveled to her lips, and she leaned against the fence, trying to block out the image of what it might feel like to kiss this handsome man.

Their eyes met and they shared a smile at the memory of riling up Myles. It had been so easy sometimes.

"Thank you for…" There were so many things on her list she didn't know what to mention first. Starting

17

with the fact that he could look past the stigma of her being a former beauty queen, and might actually believe she had a few rocks rattling around in her head. But even bigger than that was that he'd stood up for her. He'd believed in, and trusted her ability to do this new job—a big and important one. One that would undoubtedly reflect on him and the team in some pretty big ways.

"Yeah," he said, looking bashful, "don't worry about it. Us Sweetheart Creekers have to stick together." He gave her a friendly nudge, then leaned against the fence beside her, his back to the party. He was so close, his arm brushed hers. What would it feel like to be held by him, to place her arms around those broad shoulders and lean in, hear his heartbeat through his shirt and all that muscle?

He idly held a bottle of beer in his hands, picking at its label. Daisy-Mae figured the drink was a prop to ward off drink offers, seeing as the hockey season had started three weeks ago.

"Well, I appreciate you vouching for me. A lot."

"Just keep me out of tutus and tiaras and we'll call it even." He gave her a smile that felt all-knowing. Like they were friends. Like they could keep each other's secrets and had inside jokes to laugh at. Which they were, and they did. But they didn't hang out together without Myles. And now that Myles was getting married, she didn't foresee many more moments like this with Maverick unless it was at a work function.

She smiled and clinked her bottle against his. "It's a deal."

"I'm still not sure what we'll do with you at the rink, though."

Her heart dropped. "What do you mean?"

"You're an incredible distraction to the players."

She laughed, his smile warming her belly. Maverick

18

thought she was beautiful. Somehow that meant more than any of her beauty queen tiaras or crowns.

He grimaced. "What? It's true. We haven't won a single game this season."

"That's not my fault! I'm not even there for the away games." She playfully jabbed a finger into his chest, secretly loving how little resistance there was. The man was fit, and she wanted to touch him all over to see where the muscles ran and where they ended.

"So how are you going to do it all?" he asked.

"Do what?" She took a sip of her beer.

"Don't you run a few businesses here in town?"

She shook her head, bending to pet Myles's dog Buckey as she came over for a scratch behind the ears. "Not anymore. I gave them up." Working home games, and now in the Dragons' offices as well, she didn't have the time to keep them up so she'd sold or closed them all down. She'd started a lot of small businesses over the years, but the daily grind of building and maintaining them was so boring they'd never really gone anywhere. It was one of the things she loved about her current job. She came up with the ideas and set them in motion, and then someone else dealt with the details of it all.

Maverick was looking at her like she was crazy. "All of them? You're not even filling in at The Watering Hole?"

She shook her head. It was a little scary letting all of those income streams go after the way they'd taken care of her over the years. Working for one company— one boss—was something she'd promised herself she'd never do again. Years ago she'd had a great job in a high-end restaurant where the tips were amazing. But when she'd talked to her boss about how he kept putting his hand on her butt, she suddenly found herself getting fewer and fewer shifts until she'd had to re-sign and find something new.

"Wow. That's a big deal." Maverick slid an arm across her shoulders, pulling her in for a brief, friendly embrace.

Movement and a flash to her right caught her attention.

"Who's that with the camera?"

MAVERICK CAST his gaze in the direction Daisy-Mae was looking. The photographer. He'd forgotten all about him as soon as he'd joined her at the fence. He'd been caught up in her dazzling smile, the easy jokes, and the fact that she'd seemingly reinvented herself in three short weeks. Gone were the cropped shirts and that certain something that screamed Texan country babe. She was still a babe, of course, and wearing her usual hat, boots, and fitted jeans. But something was different. Was it her top? Hair? Makeup? She had a so-phisticated nuance now that put her in a whole new category of The Sexiest Woman On Earth.

He rubbed his forehead, trying to refocus his thoughts. Daisy-Mae was a massive distraction.

She was also unattainable. And therefore perfectly fine to have a slight obsession over as long as they didn't spend much time together so she didn't pull him from what truly mattered—the game.

But that didn't mean he couldn't still imagine having Daisy-Mae on his arm, taking her out to the nicest restaurants in the city and pampering her. He'd bet, despite her many pageant wins, that no man had ever treated her the way she truly deserved. Not even his best friend, Myles Wylder, who'd cared deeply for her. The two had stayed together beyond their teenage years more out of habit than love or deep compatibility. And for some reason, it was often Maverick reminding Myles that Daisy-Mae had a birthday coming up, or that Valentine's Day was just around the corner. That shouldn't happen. Especially to a woman as special and loyal as Daisy-Mae.

"The PR team has him shadowing me," Maverick said, finally clearing his thoughts enough to answer her earlier question.

"Why?"

"They're hoping to catch some candid shots of me being a decent human being, I guess." He tried to play it off like his reputation didn't bother him. Although he was sure she'd heard just how severely his crappy reputation was dragging down the team and maybe even knew more about the team's plans to fix it than he did.

"He took a photo of us."

Maverick nodded. He wanted to laugh and enjoy that sunshine smile of hers, not talk about this. When he'd shot down the fairy-tale idea he'd had to agree to something. So a trailing photographer it was.

"Why? Are you going to be in an article or something?" Her look grew wary as she sized up the photographer.

"Do you want me to go over there and crush his camera?"

A mischievous twinkle flashed in her blue eyes. "Would you do that for me?"

"Anything."

"Great. I could use another beer." She handed him her empty bottle.

He hesitated, unsure whether he was being tested, teased, or if she simply just wanted a fresh drink.

"Sure. Same kind?" He checked the label. Not a Wylder homemade brew made by the youngest brother Ryan—smart call.

"Yes, please." He moved away. "Oh, and can you get me some of Maria's layered dip?"

Her request was innocent enough on the surface, but he knew getting his hands on Maria's dip at a party where her octogenarian father-in-law Carmichael was present was like trying to fill a water glass in the middle of a desert.

Maverick scanned the people clustered under the *Congratulations Myles and Karen* banner. Sure enough, Carmichael was there, hunched over the layered dip, elbows out like he was ready to bite anyone who dared try to take a scoop.

"Get some yourself," he told her with a light scoff.

"So much for doing *anything* for me." She gave him a dramatic roll of her eyes.

He snorted and headed to the beer trough near the patio's smoking barbecue. He bumped into Myles along the way, and they walked back to the fence together.

"Look who I found," Maverick said to Daisy-Mae.

"Lovely party," she told Myles. Her smile didn't emit her usual ray of sunshine, and Maverick figured it had to be pretty tough being here. She and Myles had sort of fizzled out over recent years, but she'd been like one of the family. Seeing her friend take the spot she must have assumed would be hers had to hurt. Or maybe it was just awkward.

"Your beer, m'lady." He bowed and handed her the bottle.

"Where's my dip?" She gestured like she was upset, playing it up.

"When are you two getting married?" Myles asked, laughing.

Maverick winced at Myles and his lack of sensitivity. Why Daisy-Mae, a smart and beautiful woman, ever went for this knucklehead was beyond Maverick. Sure, his friend was charming and caring. But he'd never been the right man for Daisy-Mae.

"Mav has cold feet," Daisy-Mae said, sliding her arm through his. That twinkle was back. Time to tease Myles. "Thanks for the beer, honey." She rolled up onto her tiptoes in her cowboy boots, planting a kiss on Maverick's cheek and spreading warmth through his entire body.

He grinned at Myles, ready for his friend's reaction, focusing on that rather than how good Daisy-Mae's soft lips had felt against his skin, how he loved being called honey.

"Well, it's about time," Myles said with something bordering on disgust.

"Sorry, what?" Maverick said as Daisy-Mae's arm went slack.

"You two. You've been over here having your own private party all night, laughing and stuff."

Daisy-Mae had fully pulled away now, and Maverick wished she'd come back, snuggle in again. "We were joking around."

"And I'm saying y'all would make a good pair." He grinned, and Maverick wondered if he was serious or if he'd finally turned the tables on them and their teasing.

Myles tipped his hat to them and headed to the patio to greet a new party arrival.

"That was weird," Daisy-Mae said. Maverick nodded.

"You know," he said, gesturing toward Myles who had found Karen and was giving her a kiss, "maybe it's just all of this disgusting happiness around us, but it almost makes me want to give it a whirl."

Daisy-Mae gave a choked laugh of surprise. "Really?"

"Sure. It might be a good thing."

Although something as consuming as marriage still

felt impossible. Daisy-Mae often referred to him as The One-Date Wonder for a solid reason. It took him a while to trust, and he'd had a lot of bad first dates thanks to his reservations. Being mildly famous, you were never sure if a woman was interested in you or what you might be able to offer. Then there was the other problem of the intense busyness during the season. Not many women enjoyed coming second to his career.

"Marriage would be a good thing how? You need a nice wifey to pack your suitcase for all your away games?"

He shot her a dark look. "No, the PR twins think marriage might help my reputation." There. Let's see what she had to say about that.

Daisy-Mae turned to study him. "Would you?"

"Get married?"

"For work and positive press?"

He shrugged, not looking at her. He'd spent the past few weeks considering the idea. There were some fatal flaws, though. First, who would he marry? Second, a marriage for show sounded like a terrible plan.

"Maybe," he admitted.

"Maybe! *Maybe?*"

A few people from the patio turned to look their way.

"It's that bad?" she asked, her eyes round.

He shrugged again and jammed his free hand into his jeans pocket.

"Wow," she said softly. "That sucks."

"Yeah."

"And it's not even your fault."

"I know." Maverick froze. Wait one second. He turned to look at her more fully. "Sorry? Say that again?"

"Well, that thing in Lafayette was obviously not

your fault. You'd never..." Her cheeks went red. The urge to kiss her was even stronger than the time she'd had it out with some pageant protesters. He'd been taken with how her face had glowed with righteous indignation. That same glow was back along with her fight. Man, it was sexy.

"Never what?" he asked, holding his breath. He felt like she knew him, saw him. Knew he'd only done something good and was paying the price repeatedly.

"You're not the type to mess up someone's marriage." She was watching him, and the party disappeared, the evening closing in around them. It was just them and this moment and the truth that so few could see but that Daisy-Mae seemed to. "I know you don't— didn't—love her. And her husband is..." She shivered.

"Is what?" He was desperate for her to intuitively understand the truth, the things he'd never spoken out loud. That she would just know because she *knew* him. Knew what he was and was not capable of.

"Adwin's not a good man. I think you were trying to help Reanna somehow."

The entire world seemed to lift from his shoulders, his chest, his mind. It was as though he could expand his ribs and inhale fully for the first time since he'd stepped in and stopped Adwin from hurting Reanna.

Daisy-Mae's cool hand rested on his and he met her eyes, hit with the force of one thought: It should never have been Myles with Daisy-Mae. It should have been him.

DAISY-MAE'S CRUSH was taking on a life of its own as she continued to hang out with Maverick. She'd always thought he was cute, but tonight, the way he was hanging out alone with her at Myles's party and laughing with her, getting honest and deep... It was messing with her mind.

It felt good to be around him. Too good, because the man was seriously out of her league. Plus, it felt wrong to crush on one of her ex's best friends. There was so much potential for broken friendships and awkward moments.

But Myles' offhand comment about her and Maverick had hurt, and she couldn't figure out why. Whatever it was, it was bringing up old feelings of being inadequate. It was as though Myles had announced to Maverick, right there in front of her, "Yeah, I don't need her anymore. She was my reserve girlfriend. I kept her on a string in case I couldn't find anyone else. But I'm good now, so you can have her."

Obviously, her mind was an absolute mess because she was certain he hadn't intended that.

It didn't help that she'd just witnessed Myles drop a kiss on Karen's waiting lips. She didn't feel jealous though. It was more like a sinking, hollow feeling as though she'd never have love—the real kind. Her dad did his best to avoid her mother. Her grandma and grandpa had separate bedrooms and had bickered all their lives. Marriage ran in her family, but love didn't. Not that burning, all-consuming kind of love that she'd been sold on by the media. The love she wanted.

But seriously. How long did a woman have to wait for true love? At this rate, she was going to be in dentures and leakproof panties by the time Cupid got down to Daisy-Mae Ray on his list.

She was still standing by the fence with Maverick, too chicken to join the party, as well as enjoying monopolizing his company. She feared he'd eventually wander off with his photographer to get some candid shots of him cuddling Myles's dog or something and she'd be forced to mingle. And if she did, it was likely that at least one person would make a remark about her missing out with Myles, and didn't it hurt to be there?

She watched the happy couple across the yard, laughing, smiling, kissing. Daisy-Mae shook her head. They'd be getting married in a few short months, on Valentine's Day. "I can't imagine it."

"Marriage?"

She tipped her head to the side, realizing she could imagine marriage. It was just the getting there from here part. "I mean, maybe I can. It would be nice to have someone to come home to. Someone who lights up when he wakes up beside me each morning."

"I thought you had a dog."

She laughed. "Ella's a girl."

"So she doesn't count?"

"Anything with four legs doesn't."

"How about someone who calls out to you when you come home? You want that? I think it would feel less lonely. Kind of like when you're a kid and your mom is happy to see that you're home from school."

"Well, Ella has that covered."

This time he laughed. "I really need to look into getting a dog."

She quirked her head at this insight into Maverick. He was lonely too? She supposed he didn't keep a girlfriend long enough to fill the void.

"You can tell your dog anything and they won't judge you for it."

"Sold!" he exclaimed, raising an arm like he was at an auction. "I'm away a lot though. That could be a problem."

They were silent for a moment.

"I need a human," Daisy-Mae said. "Meals, road trips... Someone to lean against while watching TV."

"That sounds pretty nice. It's hard to find someone you don't mind in your space."

Was that why his new ranch outside of town had been declared, unofficially, a woman-free zone? His mom was there frequently, by the sounds of things, but that was it. Myles had tried to explain that it was Maverick's sanctuary when Daisy-Mae and Karen protested on behalf of womankind when they'd wanted to tag along and see the place. Naturally, it had only made Daisy-Mae even more curious about what had gone on with Maverick and Reanna, and before that, Janie.

Silence stretched between them, pleasant and comfortable. The party was growing louder, and a burst of laughter echoed across the yard.

"You know, most people date a little longer than sixteen months before getting married," Maverick pointed out, resting an elbow on the fence, looking at Daisy-Mae.

"No, they don't."

"Okay, true. But these two were as good as engaged after four months of dating."

"I can't imagine being engaged in four months from now. There are literally no contenders."

"None? You lie."

"I do not!"

"You're smart, kind, gorgeous, sassy, and fun. You have men lined up waiting for you to notice them."

She snorted.

"Daisy-Mae," he said, his tone serious, "you have a full NHL team roster waiting to date you."

"A roster full of flirts, you mean?" She crossed her arms. "Because not a soul has asked me out."

Maverick looked away with a hint of guilt. "Yeah, that's strange."

"Anyway, I need someone who'll love me just the way I am. No changes required."

"It really shouldn't be difficult. People get married all the time. It's easy."

"Then why aren't you hitched to some power-babe?" she retorted.

"I will if you will."

"With you?"

Maverick clinked his beer bottle against hers. "You just called shotgun on me. Congratulations. There'll be a prenup on your desk by Monday morning. You do have a desk now, right?"

She pulled her beer away from his and gave him a scowl that was difficult to master thanks to the giant smile that kept slipping out. "You think you're so funny."

She took a swallow of her drink, trying to hide the way her face was burning at the thought of marrying Maverick. To have a man like him... all hers? Mind. Blown.

"Why not?" he asked, leaning closer in the growing twilight. "I have money, looks..."

She simply raised her brows.

He laughed with a casual shrug. "Myles gave us the all-clear."

For a second, right before he laughed again, she thought she detected a hint of seriousness.

MAVERICK WAS HALF serious about marrying Daisy-Mae. She was the kind of woman who might understand his insane schedule and not shy away from the occasional bit of fame and recognition that came with his career. Plus, he really enjoyed hanging out with her.

Daisy-Mae's expression darkened, and she gestured subtly to something behind him. About eight feet away was Henry Wylder. Myles's great-uncle and the grumpiest, unhappiest man in the town's long history.

And he was talking to Maverick's mom.

"At least he's not after us," Daisy-Mae said. "But maybe we should save her somehow? He has a way of making you feel like the smallest, least significant, and stupidest person in the world."

"Henry still hasn't forgiven me for warping his great-nephews. He likes to remind her of that."

"Oh, the hockey thing?" Daisy-Mae frowned. "Really?"

Myles and his brothers had gotten into hockey alongside Maverick as teens, hitching rides to the city to skate on the only ice for miles. Henry had felt they were shirking their responsibilities on the ranch and that Maverick was tempting the boys into believing in a dream that would never come true for them. It probably irked him most that Maverick had made it, and not one of his kin.

But had that short-lived passion for hockey caused the Wylder brothers any long-lasting damage? No. Had it been amazing for all of them? Yes.

"My Lafayette *scandal* hasn't exactly helped his opinion of me, especially now that I'm 'tainting' the town with my presence. It's enough that my mom has to read about the lies, but having someone like Henry rail at her about it is too much."

Daisy-Mae was chewing on the inside of her cheek, a sure sign something was bothering her. "You should rescue her."

Maverick gave her elbow a squeeze. He moved a few steps away but hesitated as Daisy-Mae's mother hustled over, all tight clothes and high heels despite the lawn party.

"Daisy-Mae! Daisy-Mae! I got the name of that surgeon I saw on that show last week." She waved a slip of paper, tipping every so often as one of her heels sunk into the dry, packed dirt. "He's expensive, but he'll be worth it."

What on earth was she up to now? She was in what Daisy-Mae had once called pageant mode, which was characterized by a slightly crazed shine in her eyes. He'd seen a few moms like that in hockey over the years, but they were nothing compared to Mrs. Ray.

"Hello, ma'am," Maverick said as the woman approached.

Daisy-Mae waved him away, clearly embarrassed. "Go save your mom."

Not a chance. He had to know what this was about. His mom could handle herself. So could Daisy-Mae, but he was infinitely more interested in what Mrs. Ray thought Daisy-Mae needed than what Henry might rant about.

"You look as lovely as ever," Maverick said to Mrs. Ray.

"Don't sweet talk me, hon," she replied, brushing him off. "It won't work."

Daisy-Mae refused to take the piece of paper thrust at her. "Mom, I told you no."

"Everything okay?" Maverick asked.

"Henry's turning red," Daisy-Mae replied, not looking away from her mom.

Indeed, Henry was in full rant. His poor mom's smile had hardened like concrete, her cheeks pink with anger. The man's gray and white hair waved in the breeze as he shook a finger, and Maverick had a feeling his mom was finally going to deliver a well-deserved verbal smackdown. He just hoped the man didn't have a heart attack and ruin her big moment.

"You're on TV now," Daisy-Mae's mom was saying. "You need to freshen things up a bit." She reached out like she was going to pat the underside of Daisy-Mae's chin, but Daisy-Mae deflected her. "Otherwise, how are you *ever* going to find a man? You're not getting any younger, you know."

"Mom, enough," Daisy-Mae warned.

"Remember when your waist was just itty-bitty?" She grabbed Maverick's arm. "Maverick, tell her."

"She looks pretty darn gorgeous to me," he said, dropping his voice low so it took on a hint of something that could be catalogued as longing.

Mrs. Ray harrumphed. "Well, you've proven you're not discerning."

"*Mom!*"

"I've been watchin' the TV. Now, Maverick hon, be a good boy and tell her what kind of fancy man she'll be missing out on with this new job if she doesn't put the effort in."

"They're all no-good men like me, Mrs. Ray."

That set her back for approximately three seconds. "But they're rich. And Daisy-Mae is in her thirties. She can't afford to be choosy."

"*Mom.*"

"Find someone nice enough"—her mother adjusted Daisy-Mae's long hair—"and accidentally forget to take your birth control. Then you'll be set for life."

Daisy-Mae visibly cringed. "That's called entrapment."

Maverick had never seen her look so humiliated and embarrassed. Not even the time her dress snagged while going down some stairs in a pageant and she took a huge tumble that cost her the crown.

He'd raced up on stage, Myles hot on his heels. It was only when he'd scooped her into his arms that he'd realized his error. She wasn't his girlfriend, and he'd just destroyed her chance at a crown-saving recovery.

"Henry Wylder," his mother's voice sounded out, catching his attention. "You need to find some woman to love you and melt that nasty, judgmental heart of yours! I do not care what you think and we are *done* talking." His mother marched off, Henry's mouth opening and closing as he hurried after her, finger wagging.

She whirled, glaring at the old man. "I won't say it again, Henry. So back off."

She glared at him for a moment longer, then stalked away, shoulders back.

Daisy-Mae's wide eyes met Maverick's and she gave a huff of surprised laughter. "Wow."

Maverick nodded. Henry had just bought himself a one-way ticket to his mother's doghouse.

"Daisy-Mae's got to take whatever's offered," Mrs. Ray continued as though the disruption hadn't occurred, "or she'll be alone forever. And this new job will be just like all the others. It won't last and she'll be home livin' with me, and I like to keep the remote all to myself when her daddy's out on the road. Beauty queens can't succeed in business. They've got to take the takin' while the takin' is good. There might not be another opportunity like this."

"Daisy-Mae's just selective, Mrs. Ray," Maverick said, doing his best not to growl. "She'll find a great man and settle down soon."

"That's just a nice way of saying nobody'll take her."

"I'd take her." He winked at Daisy-Mae, wishing she knew how true that was. Especially now that Myles seemed to have waved the checkered flag, possibly removing the Bro Code clause that had kept him from asking her out.

CHAPTER 3

*M*averick dropped an article on Louis's desk in the small office just off the locker room. "What's going on?"

Maverick's hands were shaking, and the feeling of betrayal stung deep.

Louis barely even glanced at the printout. He leaned back in his chair, watching Maverick.

"Wait..." Maverick said slowly. Louis knew about the photos of Maverick with Daisy-Mae and wasn't upset. The photographer had been hired by the team... So that meant...

Maverick placed the heels of his hands against his temples and pushed. This was bad. Really bad. He folded his two-hundred-and-ten-pound build into the chair across from Louis. In hockey, he was considered big. But in this office that smelled faintly of locker room, sitting in this stupid trendy leather chair, he felt even bigger, like nothing fit right. He bent over, trying to quiet his racing mind.

"Tell me you didn't authorize this." He peered upward long enough to see Louis swallow, his Adam's apple bobbing. He looked like that man Maverick had cornered in a bar for harassing the waitress.

"I approved the photos, yes."

Maverick slumped. He hadn't expected this. Not from Louis.

His coach sat up straighter. "If you won't tell everyone what really happened in Lafayette, then the team has to do what it has to do."

Maverick exploded out of his seat, arms in the air. "This is as bad as before with all the lies and deceit." He pointed in the direction of Lafayette, his old team, the press that had hounded him. He was shouting and someone closed the office door. "Telling the world that Daisy-Mae and I are an item—" His mind froze for a second. He'd seen her earlier in the day and she'd been hands-down sexy in her new work wardrobe, giving him long, heated glances that made him want to hit the elevator's Stop button and mess up her lipstick.

There had been no hint in her quiet body language that she was upset about anything. There'd been no dragging him out of the elevator and demanding he explain himself, the photos, the article, this entire crazy corporation.

"Have you even spoken to her?" he asked.

Louis stroked his neck like he did when he was stressed about a high-stakes game. "Maverick," he said evenly, "it's been months of this mess following you around. I talked to you about doing something about it at the beginning of the season. We're into November now and you haven't made any moves to make this better. The PR team saw an opportunity, and we took it."

"Nobody cleared this with her? You set us up." She was going to be justifiably angry.

Louis sighed.

"Well, I'm sure you can expect Daisy-Mae in your office at any moment. And yes, yours. She's not dumb." He crossed his arms. "You dragged her into *my* mess without asking her if she wanted to be tainted by all of this. She's just starting out here. This could impact her career. Did you think about that?"

He felt sick to his stomach. You didn't treat friends this way. You protected them.

Louis cleared his throat, toying with the pens on his desk. "I think this could be a good thing." He wouldn't look at Maverick.

"It's finally come down to money mattering most, hasn't it? What if I say no to all of this? Are you going to fire me?"

"Maybe." Louis shifted forward in his seat.

He felt his jaw slacken as he realized how serious Louis was. The man had always been in his corner. Always.

He sagged into his abandoned chair.

"What if I deny this?" He pointed to the article. It was mostly photos. A few lines about him, Daisy-Mae, their friendship and careers. His throat tightened, and the walls felt like they were pressing in on him. He wanted these photos to be true. He wanted what this article was selling.

"I don't think anyone will believe you," Louis said quietly, as though embarrassed by voicing the truth.

"I thought this photographer you had shadow me was supposed to help."

Louis spun the papers, shoving them Maverick's way. "Look."

"I already have."

"No. Impartially. Objectively. Not as some alpha trying to protect the woman you have the hots for."

Geez. Was he that transparent?

Reluctantly Maverick obeyed and pulled the papers off the desk. He didn't want to look at the photos, didn't want to admit to himself or to Louis that he was cornered and possibly facing the end of his career if he didn't accept the sudden change of rules.

"This is literally the only helpful stuff he got after tailing you for almost two weeks. You're a hermit."

"I thought everyone told me to lay low," he grumbled.

The first shot in the article was of Daisy-Mae leaning in at Myles's party. Her long hair was tickling his sleeve, and both of them were smiling as though sharing a private joke. He remembered that moment. She was dishing it back after he'd teased her about the promotion. The look she'd given him when she'd realized he'd helped her had hit him hard in the gut. Her expression had suggested nobody had ever helped her out like that. Which couldn't possibly be true. But it made him want to help her all the more.

He curled the papers into a tube in his hands. "The staff won't take her seriously if they think she's dating me."

"Why not?"

"It'll look like nepotism. Like you hired my girlfriend."

"They hired her before this article says you started dating."

He uncurled the pages. "Or they'll call her a puck bunny. Or…" He looked at the photos again. Daisy-Mae wasn't wearing her usual sexy attire. It was more subdued. She was wearing cowboy boots, hat, and jeans, but her shirt covered more skin than normal. She looked like a beautiful professional woman who held an amazing position on the team.

Which meant she was dating a dumb jock. He was the one punching above his dating grade.

Maverick exhaled and rubbed his face, trying to collect his thoughts. He felt like he didn't know which way was up any longer. This whole thing was a violation, but every argument he reached for failed to help him make his case.

"Look…" Louis's voice was soft in a way that caused Maverick's guard to go up. "You're both in your thirties. If love hasn't happened for either of you, what's the harm in a small masquerade for the betterment of the team?"

Maverick popped out of his seat, tossing the article on Louis's desk. "I can find my own date, thank you."

"You don't like her?"

"She's a friend." He towered over Louis's desk, pushing the tip of his finger against its smooth surface. "And I'm not going to ask her to have a fake relationship with me. I won't tie her up so she can't find the love of her life. My problems are not her responsibility."

If love happened between them, he'd welcome it. But not like this. This wasn't an honest way to start a relationship, and with Daisy-Mae he wanted nothing but the real thing.

Louis shifted the papers, pointing to the photo on the second page. Daisy-Mae was looking at Maverick like she wanted him to kiss her. How the photographer had gotten that close without them noticing he had no clue. Had they really been that wrapped up in each other's worlds?

He didn't need an answer to that. Any time Daisy-Mae stepped into the room, he forgot everything. Even hockey.

"You two obviously like each other. What's the problem with riding this wave?"

"It's a lie."

"I can set up a press conference so you can call me a liar in public to make yourself feel better, but nobody's going to believe it. In fact, this story is already running in a few places." Louis's voice lowered even though Maverick had moved further away, toward the door. "And the press is actually positive for once."

38

Maverick halted, hope and his righteousness battling each other. The world wanted to see him with Daisy-Mae?

"As well, several agents have received calls this morning. The good kind."

Sponsorship deals for rookies? He turned to face Louis. The man was serious.

"Coincidental," he said, dismissing the idea of his article being connected. "It's too soon for anyone to change their mind about me or the team and start offering deals."

Louis slowly shook his head, and Maverick came back to sit across from Louis's desk. Suddenly this may no longer only be a matter of pride or protecting Daisy-Mae from the disaster of his life.

He glanced through the pages of photos again. He and Daisy-Mae looked like the real deal. But why was the public loving this?

Because Daisy-Mae was beautiful and glowing, and he looked like he'd do anything for her.

It looked like love.

He sighed. "I don't know what to do with any of this, but you're the one who has to explain this all to Daisy-Mae and figure it out."

The office door flew open and there was his pretend girlfriend, flushed, her forehead creased. She was wearing a fitted white blouse, black slacks with a zipper up the side, and heeled ankle boots with a white rose stitched into the black leather. Maverick didn't think he'd ever seen a woman looking as tall—or as angry—as Daisy-Mae Ray. There was a fire in her eyes, and her body was taking up more space than Landon protecting his net. He swore he heard Louis gulp.

Despite how twisted it might make him, Maverick hoped he left this meeting with Daisy-Mae as his girlfriend.

"REALLY? *REALLY?*" Daisy-Mae marched over to Louis's desk, ignoring Maverick who had sat up straight when she'd arrived. "Do you not ask your photographers to sign something when you hire them so they can't release photos without approval?"

"Daisy-Mae, I…"

"What? You're sorry your photographer sold out the man he was hired to help?"

What if Maverick believed that she'd slipped a few bills to the cameraman and asked him to make up this story? It wouldn't be a giant leap for anyone after the way her mom had announced at Myles's party that Daisy-Mae should entrap a player. The only question would be why the photographer took so long to sell her story.

"Well, actually…"

"Is this some sort of ill-informed publicity stunt? You're a coach, not in PR. Because this is the opposite of what Maverick needs! You're supposed to coach him. And when you're not doing that, protect and help him." She turned to Maverick, who was watching her attentively. "You need to call your agent because this is pure crap."

Maverick pointed to Louis, forehead creasing.

"What?" she demanded, turning back to Louis.

"The press has actually been quite positive about the idea of the two of you dating."

She cleared her throat, trying to act like that little fact didn't completely blast through her resolve to stay angry. She wanted to melt, sit down and ask for a full retelling of the public's reaction.

"It's a lie!" She turned to Maverick. "Unless I missed you asking me out at some point?"

His hands were clasped between his knees, and his

lips were pulled into a frown. He looked calm, steady. And incredibly hot in his jeans and pressed white shirt. The dampness in his hair from his post-workout shower. That chin. That jawline. The depth of his gaze which kept pulling her into his orbit.

Her mind wanted to race down dangerous avenues that were definitely not open to traffic. Little did this man know that he was one of her biggest fantasies. She'd be over the moon if this article told the truth and he'd chosen her.

"Have a seat." Louis gestured to the chair beside Maverick. She paused for a second, but Maverick shrugged, not looking nearly as perturbed as she thought he should.

"You two look natural together," Louis said. "Everyone can see it."

"We're *friends*." Daisy-Mae wrapped her arms around herself, cursing herself for flirting with him so steadily at the party. "This is…is slanderous or some-thing! It's defrauding the public, and it's going to make Maverick look even worse when the truth comes out."

Beside her, Maverick was grinning.

"What?" Daisy-Mae flashed him a look. He was not helping his case at all. He should be more upset than she was. It was *his* reputation at stake.

"I've never had anyone defend me like this. It's sexy."

"Well, it's about time someone did." She turned back to Louis, long finger extended at him. "How are you going to fix this?"

"I'm not in the PR department!" He raised his hands in surrender.

"They told me *you* approved and collaborated. That makes all of this your problem."

Louis gave a small cough and shot Maverick an alarmed look. He sat a little straighter. "Define fix."

Daisy-Mae blinked, unsure. This was about where

her anger and plan ran out. Her and her loud mouth. "You tell me."

"This was an attempt to help Maverick," Louis stated carefully. "It wasn't anyone's intention when the photographer was hired to make up a relationship, but we can't deny the fact that it's been less than twenty-four hours since it went live, and it's helping."

"You..." Daisy-Mae couldn't find the words. She looked at Maverick. His eyes were closed, and it appeared as though he was doing some deep breathing techniques.

"The papers are loving it. It's spreading like wildfire and everyone wants to know who you are." Louis sat back, looking rather pleased with himself.

Daisy-Mae was itching to learn more, but she stayed focused on her waning anger.

"So now we're a thing?" Daisy-Mae said, a hint of disgust in her tone that she hadn't meant. She wanted Maverick to *choose* her. Not get stuck with her. When he kissed her—if he kissed her—she wanted it to be real. She wanted to feel whatever she felt with him without the constant thought he was just faking it all. And this—this would all be fake from start to finish.

"Hey, I'm a catch, you know," Maverick grumbled from beside her.

"I *know*." Daisy-Mae barely glanced at him, her focus on Louis. "But this is manipulative!"

"Have you looked at the article, Daisy-Mae?" Louis asked carefully. "Really looked at it?"

He pushed a printout closer, and she hazarded a peek. Earlier, when she'd first saw the photos, she hadn't recognized herself. But it was no wonder everyone thought they were an item. She was leaning way too close to Maverick. And that look she was giving him? Wow. Lovesick much? She was like a cartoon heroine swooning over a hero.

She swallowed, more than a little embarrassed, and glanced at Louis, then back to the article. In these photos she looked like someone. Someone she'd always wanted to be. Someone who dated highflyers and belonged with them.

A few weeks ago she'd ducked into Jenny's shop in Sweetheart Creek to find something that said Serious Professional Woman Working in the City. She'd found a few items but then had ended up in San Antonio with some friends, one of them the best designer bargain shopper ever, Mandy Mattson from Blueberry Springs. It was a good thing her friend lived way up north because they'd given Daisy-Mae's credit card a healthy workout. One it couldn't afford to do very often. But she'd found that amazing balance between sexy and professional. Fitted blouses, black pants, and heels for work. But with a classy, sexy twist, and some Texas style. Some of her makeover had spilled over into her casual wardrobe as well. And judging by these photos, the makeover had done the trick. She had finally outgrown her trailer park roots and arrived. And she'd arrived with Maverick Blades leaning in, his shoulder pressed against hers, smiling like he adored her.

Had he known ahead of time that this fake article was going to be leaked? Had he been instructed to find a mark at the party and she'd willingly swooned when given his undivided attention?

"I want what's best for Maverick," she said softly, pushing the papers back at Louis. "He's a good man. A friend."

She forced herself not to say more, to believe that he wasn't behind this.

"This is helping Maverick and our team," Louis said, gesturing to the article. "Rookies couldn't get deals, but their phones are ringing today. Because of this."

There was no way that could be true. Daisy-Mae glanced at Maverick. He nodded.

"Fans seem to like seeing you together." Louis slid a piece of paper across his desk.

It was a printout from social media. A photo of her with Dezzie Dragon in the players' box during a practice with Maverick leaning over the gate to chat with her. Both of them were full of smiles. Someone had snapped it during an open-to-the-public practice while she and Violet had been practicing moving around the arena. The headline said "I knew it!"

"Can I see?" Maverick asked, reaching for the page. He glanced at it, his expression softening. "Remind me to follow this account." He placed the photo back on Louis's desk.

"Nice to see something positive for once, huh?" Louis smiled at Maverick who nodded.

"This isn't true though," Daisy-Mae pointed out.

"Fighting or denying this may make a bigger mess for Maverick," Louis warned.

"So what do we do?"

"Why don't the two of you consider this?" Louis said amicably. "Go out for supper—"

"So you can have more photos taken?" Maverick asked.

"Yeah?" Daisy-Mae backed him up.

"And the team will pay the tab as an apology," he said in a calm tone no doubt meant to soothe their ruffled feathers. "You both work hard for the Dragons. And if nothing else, you can celebrate the fact that one rookie was already offered a sponsorship deal on the tail of this news." Louis tapped the papers on his desk. "Ultimately, what you decide to do in your private lives is none of the team's business."

But what if dating Maverick was part of her new contract? One of those clauses that weren't written down because they were illegal but would be reinforced by her contract not being renewed if she didn't play nicely?

And if it was decided that they should continue this public ruse, hanging out with Maverick like they were a couple wouldn't exactly cramp her style or any immediate dating plans.

"Wait." Daisy-Mae ran Louis's words through her head again. "You're saying that rookies weren't getting deals? But this has only been out for a few hours..."

"The sponsor asked about the two of you."

"And you said what?" Maverick asked.

"The PR team informed them that neither of you are married, and that you've been friends since you were kids. They ate it up." He shrugged again. "You two look good together and have that magic everyone can see."

"But..." There had to be a clincher of a reason to say absolutely no to this crazy idea. She turned to Maverick. "What if true love comes along, but you're pretending to date me?"

"I doubt that would be a problem." He wouldn't look at her.

"Why?"

He was silent for a long beat. "Because I'm unlucky in love."

"No. You're fussy. You barely even dated in high school."

"I've always been busy with hockey—which is where I *am* lucky. I can't have a horseshoe with me in every area of my life. It's difficult to find someone who understands my lifestyle."

"You're fussy."

"Fine. I'm fussy. I'm searching for the right princess to wear the glass slipper I keep in my back pocket." The way he looked at her seized her lungs. It felt like he was

45

carrying that slipper for her, waiting for her to extend her foot. Maybe she should have said yes to the PR duo dressing her up in a princess gown.

"So. Supper. Tonight?" Louis asked, the hope in his voice clear.

"Tonight?" Maverick asked Daisy-Mae, his eyebrows lifted.

"Nobody goes on a date on Monday night," she replied, putting her proverbial foot down. A princess had to set some ground rules, after all.

Maverick gave her a slow smile of approval. "Friday?"

"Friday you have an away game."

Maverick glanced at Louis, who nodded.

"Fine, Saturday? I'm free?"

Again Louis nodded.

"I'll be all yours—any time you want."

She extended her proverbial foot for his glass slipper. "Saturday would be lovely."

"And if you can swing it," Louis said, "please come back engaged."

IF MAVERICK WAS GOING to do this, he was doing it right.

He hustled up the steps to Daisy-Mae's small house in the country. He had a rare Saturday off and had spent it working on his place a few miles from hers, slowly getting it in shape. His mom had taken point on the renovation plans, and every time they went into town, she took him down yet another aisle in the hardware store. He was doubting the wisdom of not buying a new home. But the charm and history of the eighty-year-old farmhouse and ranch had won him over in an instant.

Money pit that it was.

He'd probably checked his watch a hundred times that afternoon, worried he'd be late.

On Daisy-Mae's porch, Maverick straightened his tie, then knocked. The door swung open almost immediately, and he froze. She was drop-dead gorgeous. He'd seen her dolled up for dozens of pageants and events over the years, but this was different. This wasn't for the stage.

This was for him.

"Are those for me?" She gestured to the tulips he was holding.

He thrust them at her, then calmed himself and cleared his throat. "They are."

"Come in while I put them in water."

Maverick stepped inside, allowing his gaze to follow the sway of her hips. She was wearing a cocktail dress that was tricky to describe. It was black. But when she moved, it turned a deep blue where the material curved around her. Her feet were bare, the hem of the dress grazing the carpeted floor.

She grabbed a jar, filling it with water at the sink in a very dated looking kitchen. She swiftly chopped the stems down to size before dropping the flowers into a beautiful arrangement. Her proficiency caused him to wonder how many other men had brought her bouquets. And yet, he knew not many. She'd mostly dated Myles as far as he knew, and his friend wasn't the type to think of flowers very often. Small gifts, yes, but not so much on the flowers.

She paused over the bouquet, inhaling their scent, eyes closed in appreciation.

Her double-wide mobile home's exterior was faded from the unrelenting Texas sun, and the yard didn't look like much. But inside it was a burst of color, feminine touches giving it a warm and cozy vibe. The furniture was mismatched. A china cabinet along one wall sparkled as its small lights made a dazzling display of her pageant crowns and tiaras. Layers of those ribbon sash things winners wore were tacked up against the cabinet's back wall. The awards intermingled with ancient-looking editions of some children's classics such as *The Wizard of Oz* and *The Lion, the Witch and the Wardrobe*. He smiled, catching sight of a tiny carved frog hiding in a tiara. The Sweet County Fair. She'd taken home the princess title that day.

Daisy-Mae had done something most wouldn't have dared do and had sung Dig a Little Deeper from The Princess and The Frog movie, encouraging the audience to sing along to the chorus of the throaty R&B song. Later he'd given her the frog as a joke and tried to call her Froggy, but she'd given him such a dark look he'd stopped. He only pulled out the nickname on occasions he was feeling particularly suicidal. So not very often.

He could still recall the hurt in her expression when she'd won yet another crown at age seventeen and he'd told her she was more than a beauty queen. She hadn't taken it the right way. Not even close. He'd meant that she was more than just her amazing looks and performances. She was bright and witty, but he could see the way the world was narrowing her existence to being nothing more than a pretty face. He feared she'd marry early, settle down, and that would be it. College and travel weren't even on the horizon any longer, despite the numerous scholarships she'd won and all the plans she'd once made.

But now, with the Dragons, she was using her smarts and natural talents in a big way.

"Ready?" Daisy-Mae asked, stepping into a black pair of stilettos that matched her purse.

"Shall we?" he asked, holding the door for her.

She looked calm and collected, but he noticed her fingers trembling as they clutched her purse.

He walked her to his car, the sleek black Mustang he'd wanted as a teenager. He opened the door for her, gently holding her elbow as she got in.

She didn't brush him off, allowing him the small gentlemanly gestures. It increased his growing suspicion that nobody had ever pampered her in quite the way he felt she deserved, but that she welcomed it.

"Where are we going?" she asked.

"McKenzie's in San Antonio. I hope you don't mind the drive?" It was over an hour, their boring commute route. But there was nothing near Sweetheart Creek that was at the level of pampering he wanted to provide. And if they were going to pretend to see what it might be like to date, he wanted to show her exactly who he was and what he was willing to provide. There would be no regrets for playing his role too small. He was going to act like tonight was real and give her no reason to say no to more time together. He planned to dazzle her, sweep her off her feet, and help her forget any reason she felt they shouldn't be together.

"Wow. McKenzie's?" she said softly. She let out a slow breath, her fingers worrying the zipper on her purse.

"Have you been?" he asked.

She shook her head, looking slightly dazzled.

He shot her his finest devilish grin. "Since Louis offered to foot the bill, I figured why not, right?"

The car filled with her laughter as he hit the gas. Maverick had a feeling this was going to be the best non-date he'd ever had.

DAISY-MAE COULD GET USED to this. Maverick was at her side, his body warming her own. He gently guided her with a hand at her lower back, whispering in her ear with funny quips as they followed the maitre d' to their table in the corner. The restaurant's lighting was low, and each table held its own candle and real roses. The room was sweet with their floral scent, making their date feel like a Valentine's Day dream rather than some sort of strange business meeting with her crush.

While they discussed whether they should pursue something romantic—for the team's sake.

If this was the way it felt to be Maverick's date, then she was all in. They hadn't even sat down yet, and this was already ranking as one of her best dates.

He helped push in her chair before sitting across from her. They had laughed frequently during the drive, and his sweet compliments were still ringing in her ears. That and the image of his slightly gob-smacked look when she'd opened her door earlier.

It felt odd being on a date with Maverick, though. Finally. After years of wondering, of avoiding thinking about it because she didn't dare dream. But if she'd allowed her full dreams to unspool into something detailed, it wouldn't have compared to this.

She noticed people eyeing them, some recognizing Maverick. The waiter certainly did, and he nearly poured Daisy-Mae's wine on her, he was so flustered by serving them.

"Is it always like this?" she asked when the waiter left, gesturing to her wineglass.

"No. Does it bother you?"

She shrugged. "Not really."

"That's good. Because it's about to get weird."

"Weird?"

She turned to find Dylan O'Neill, one of the team's

players, hobbling toward them on crutches. Daisy-Mae's stomach sank.

"Is he joining us?" she whispered.

"Not a chance," Maverick said, standing to shake hands as Dylan arrived. More heads turned to take in the two NHL players.

"What's this?" Dylan asked, gesturing to Maverick's wine glass. "I thought you were off the sauce during season, old man."

"You can't let a lady drink alone," Maverick stated.

Dylan gave Daisy-Mae an incredulous look. "No, you can't let this old geezer drink. We'll never win a game."

"Y'all aren't winning games anyway," Daisy-Mae said dryly. "May as well try something new." She'd meant it as a joke, but as soon as the words left her mouth, she felt bad. The team was having a horrible season, and she should be way more supportive and encouraging.

"It's true," Maverick said with a laugh. Dylan gave a sheepish grin, the two men taking the ribbing for what it was meant to be.

"You two on a date?" Dylan asked.

"He's trying to convince me of his worthiness," Daisy-Mae said casually, loving the way Maverick played up her teasing with a loud groan.

"Well, when he fails the test, you let me know and I'll introduce you to a real man." Dylan winked.

Maverick's hands turned to fists, and he glowered at Dylan, stony-faced.

Daisy-Mae laughed as Dylan hurried away to sit with the couple he'd come in with.

"You're going to need to date me," Maverick said simply, retaking his seat.

"What?" Daisy-Mae asked, amused. It was fun having two men pretend to fight over her.

"First of all, if we're dating, then we'd no longer be lying to the world. Second, it will keep those no-good scallywags from pestering you." He nodded toward Dylan.

"Oh, so you'd be offering protection? Because it seems like you're being a date-blocker."

"I don't know what that is, but sure. It's a sacrifice I'm willing to make. They're all worthless thugs, and if I stop running interference, you'll need a big ol' hockey stick to beat them off."

"Sounds fun." She gave him a perky smile, aware she was killing him. There was no pretending: he was flirting back. And it was fun. So much fun she found herself wishing away her years with Myles so she could have gotten to this place in her life sooner.

Then again, without the efforts of trying to make love bloom with Myles, she might not fully appreciate that the way Maverick made her feel was rare and wonderful.

"You and this makeover of yours," Maverick said, his eyes running over her up-do, subtle makeup, and cocktail gown. "You're nothing but sexy trouble."

She toyed with her necklace, giving him a slow blink. "I'm a bit insulted that you feel I can't handle the attention."

"You really want a hockey player?" he asked. His elbow was on the table, and he was suddenly serious. "We're always away for games from October to Spring. Always on the ice."

"Handy."

"Handy how?" That dark look returned.

"That'll make it even easier for you to fake being a family man when you finally give in and settle down in one of these PR masquerades." She winked at him.

"So, is that a yes?"

"To faking it with you?"

He gave a brief nod.

She thought about lying to her family and friends. Her father, a trucker, would be happy she'd found someone, although maybe worried about the amount of time she and Maverick would spend apart. Her mom would brag to anyone who listened and then give her a giant I-told-you-so once they did the fake breaking up part. Her friends...her friends had done a good job of pretending not to notice she was crushing on Mr. Unattainable for the past year or two. Although Violet was no longer pretending now that she'd gotten to know Maverick a bit better. She was fully on board with Daisy-Mae's crush status, which meant she might explode with happiness for her. That could be a bit awkward.

On the flip side, it might be nice to experience having life go well for a little bit. A good job, a nice boyfriend. Not that she hadn't had that before. It just hadn't been quite on this level. This easy.

"It'll be complicated," she said at last.

"By the sounds of things, you'd really be helping out, but I understand if you don't want to."

"I'm not good at lying. I hate it, in fact."

"Me, too."

An idea came to her in a flash, and she could feel the heat hit her cheeks as she tried to summon the courage to speak it out loud.

She adjusted her cutlery, realigned her wineglass. "Maybe we could momentarily set the fake part aside and just date."

She dared to peek at Maverick. His eyes had grown rounder.

"I mean, you know... Go on dates and stuff and I'd call you my..." She sucked in a deep breath, and said, "My boyfriend. And we'd, um, maybe kiss in public sometimes?" She scrunched her nose. "You know. For publicity. But it would be dating. For real. But we couldn't break up. Not right away. We'd have to keep things up for a bit. Until everything was stable."

Maverick was nodding slowly. He had a strange look on his face and she couldn't tell if he was trying to school a smile or if he was deep in thought.

"It would help Landon," Maverick said. "He needs a deal. Cassandra—his girlfriend—her son needs heart surgery and she can't afford it."

"Cassandra McTavish? Alexa's sister? From Blueberry Creek Ranch?" Daisy-Mae felt panic like it was her own son. "Dusty's sick?" The boy was just starting school. He had so much life ahead of him. Or at least, he should.

"Yeah. Landon would like to help, but he has a lot of debt and she won't let him. If he had a big deal, she might say yes. But I don't want—"

"Okay." Daisy-Mae's voice was so firm Maverick stopped talking.

"Okay what?"

"Maverick, hon, if you'll take me, I'm officially your girlfriend."

54

CHAPTER 4

$\mathcal{M}$averick's side, where Daisy-Mae was leaning against him, felt as good as though the sun was shining on him. They had finished eating and were now strolling along the Riverwalk area downtown, the evening stretching out around them. Lights strung through the branches above twinkled as they entered under the canopy of oak trees. It was romantic, quiet.

Daisy-Mae gave him a sweet smile.

"Hey, you," he said softly, stopping on one of the wooden footbridges arching over the slow, winding river below.

She snuggled closer, tucking into him, her expression peaceful. Back in the restaurant, he'd said yes to her dating idea, of course. And so now Daisy-Mae Ray was his girlfriend. He'd had a good feeling about tonight, and so far it was exceeding his wildest dreams of what a first date could be like.

They'd agreed to a real-fake relationship where they'd stick together for several weeks or months. He didn't think anyone had ever wanted bad press and a poor reputation to last so long as he did right now. He wouldn't sabotage their efforts to help the team, but he would milk every moment to show her he thought they were meant to be together—for real.

Across the river, a similar string of lights to those hanging above them lined the edge of a restaurant patio where people were having drinks. Maverick sensed a stir, their attention turning toward the bridge where he and Daisy-Mae were cuddled together. He shifted so his back was to the group as soon as the first phone lifted to take a photo.

Daisy-Mae, sensing something was up, peeked around his shoulder. "What are you doing?"

"Habit."

"You're hiding!"

"Like I said, habit." He didn't move.

"The whole reason we're doing this is so people will see us and take photos." She shifted him so their profiles were facing the group, renewing the stir of lifted phones.

Maverick kept his focus on Daisy-Mae, the reminder of the fake element of their night stinging like a wasp.

"Sorry," he said. "It's instinct to shield you." Janie had hated the publicity of dating him, and even though they'd broken up more than four years ago, the habit of shying away still ran deep. Having bad press for the past year hadn't helped his desire to avoid being front and center, either.

But with Daisy-Mae it was more that he wanted to keep their relationship private so it could grow naturally. It was too important to him to let the public mess it up.

However, that wasn't part of the deal.

He sighed, giving in, turning to smile at the cameras. "Is this better?"

He peeked down at her. She was playing with his

shirt, smoothing it, resting her hands flat on his chest, looking up at him, smiling. Posing.

"Maybe we should kiss." She blushed, her teeth softly capturing her lower lip for a brief second.

"I don't want our first kiss to belong to everyone else." He wanted it to be just them sharing that moment.

Her body softened against his. "You're pretty romantic for a real-fake boyfriend."

"I try."

She gave him one of those sunshiny smiles that made life feel as though everything was possible. He'd never figured out why Myles hadn't tied Daisy-Mae down the first chance he'd had as a teen. It wasn't like marriage straight out of high school was unheard of around Sweetheart Creek. And she was the kind of woman who caused a man to stop thinking, make poor decisions, and let out their inner caveman. You'd swear until you were blue in the face that you'd never get married. Then she walked by and it was all you could do to slide your ring on her finger before anyone else could.

That about summed up Daisy-Mae Ray.

As a prime example, he even knew what kind of ring he'd buy her. Something classy that showed that he saw beyond her small-town roots. Something big. Bold. Beautiful. Expensive. Something that proved to her that he planned to pamper her for the rest of their days.

He cleared his throat, realizing he was firmly in troubled territory. Especially since that wasn't the first time she'd called him her real-fake boyfriend tonight.

"We're exclusive," he said, his voice coming out gruffer than he'd planned.

"Of course." She gave him a slight shove, then grabbed his arm, bringing him around her again. "Otherwise, what's the point of all of this?"

JEAN ORAM

"Right."

"I'll come to events with you and stuff like that. Like it was real." She looked bashful, very different from the take-charge Daisy-Mae he knew. Then she blasted him with one of those full smiles again that made him feel as though he'd won the Stanley Cup.

"To help the team," he said, more to remind himself than to clarify anything with her. "To make sure Louis doesn't seem like a liar and further damage my image."

She gently traced a finger down his cheek in what was simply the most seductive move he'd ever experienced. "Don't forget, you're also protecting me from the guys on your team through some misplaced sense of duty."

Man, he wished there was nobody around so he could kiss her. "Are you gonna bust my chops the whole time we date?"

She gave him a flirty little twist and was out of his arms. "Of course."

"Boy, am I ever in for it," he said, feeling the barren chill against his side where she'd been tucked.

They began walking again, down the slope of the arched bridge, away from the patio of onlookers.

"Are you sure you can handle all of this? There's still time to back out." She turned, walking backward. The bridge's boards were uneven, and she was still wearing those crazy sexy shoes. Fearing she'd tumble, Maverick caught up to her, sweeping his arms around her.

"I can definitely handle all that is Daisy-Mae Ray." They were nose to nose, the city alive around them.

She made a soft sound, and he almost kissed her, filling in the empty beat.

He gently slipped her from his arms, taking her hand and wishing they could flee back to Sweetheart Creek to carve out enough privacy so he could finally kiss her.

58

NOT WANTING the evening to end, Daisy-Mae begged Maverick to take her to a coffee shop they both knew called The Gingerbread Café. It was a few blocks from the Dragons' head office and meant their date would last at least an extra hour. Hopefully. Maverick, since being photographed during their walk, had been antsy to disappear. But as his girlfriend, she had a task. Make him look good and get the public to adore him in the way he deserved.

And stretch the date in case he woke up in the morning and realized this was all a very terrible idea.

Or the public decided they didn't like her after all.

The café was hopping. Being licensed to serve alcohol, it stayed fairly busy from open to close, especially on weekends.

"Do you want to go somewhere else?" Maverick asked over the sounds of the bustling café. "There's nowhere to sit."

"We could grab something and walk?" she suggested, the scents of gingerbread and vanilla making her hungry.

"You sure?" His gaze dropped to her high heels.

"Yeah." There was no way she was ending their evening early because of her feet.

His hand gently touched her lower back and shivers zipped down her spine as he guided her toward the counter where they could place their order.

Daisy-Mae couldn't stop smiling. She wanted to shout out that Maverick Blades had said yes to her. They were out on a date.

But it was fake. Not fully real, she reminded herself. Although almost real. Pretty much real.

Their relationship had an expiration sometime after Maverick's reputation was back on solid ground. When that would be, she didn't know, but she hoped for her own sake it would take a year or two. Or however long it took Maverick to realize he couldn't live without her.

A crowd of men chatting near the counter shifted, parting to let them through, eyeing her and her out-of-place outfit.

"Promise me something," Maverick murmured in her ear as they waited in line.

"What?"

"You'll tell me if you want out early. Any reason."

Her heart dropped. She'd been expecting a sweet something, not a reminder of why they were here in the first place.

"Of course," she said lightly, hoping her voice didn't betray her. "And you, too."

Blindly, Daisy-Mae ordered a hot drink at the long bar, the barista waving off Maverick's offer to pay. Beside them was a display of beautifully decorated gingerbread men cookies which she knew were there all year and not just when Christmas was slowly approaching.

"Daise?"

She blinked, realizing Maverick had given her a nickname. She didn't mind it. It was better than Froggy —one he'd tried on eons ago and she'd quickly squelched.

He locked his gaze on hers, sending warmth all the way down to her chilly toes. "I won't."

"Won't what?"

"Want out early."

"Oh." She nodded, her head feeling light with the firmness of his answer. "Okay."

A woman a ways down the bar was sliding closer, her eyes pinned on Maverick. "You're Maverick Blades, aren't you?"

Okay, Daisy-Mae could kind of see why the recognition thing got a bit tiring for him. Was it really like this everywhere he went? She'd never noticed it being this bad before.

The woman sat on the stool next to Maverick, one hand casually pulling the hem of her skirt higher, giving him a full view of thigh.

"He's taken," Daisy-Mae said, leaning forward to speak around him. She winced, realizing she could be overstepping. But no, they were on a date, and in the eyes of the public, he *was* taken. By her.

The woman's smile fell as she turned to Maverick for confirmation. "Are you?"

"Afraid so," he said cheerily, sliding an arm around Daisy-Mae's shoulder and planting a warm kiss on her forehead that made her knees go shaky.

He collected their orders, handing her the medium mocha and keeping the large dark roast coffee with one milk for himself.

"Does that happen often?" she asked, looking over her shoulder as he held the door for her. The flirt was pouting, watching Maverick go. Daisy-Mae knew it wasn't a terrible view. The man didn't have any bad angles.

"Does what?" Maverick's gaze was on her lips as she sipped her drink in the quiet of the sidewalk. Usually there were a few tables out front, but at this time of night they were tucked away inside. "Oh. The paying thing? My buddy Dak owns this place. I helped him find the location and such, and some of the staff know me... so..."

"No, *that*." She pointed to the building behind them. "The woman."

"Oh! Uh, yeah." He pulled the lid off his coffee and took a long drink despite its heat. "Since Lafayette."

Daisy-Mae watched him while they walked.

"That type seems to think I'm a bad boy now. They

61

usually flirt to make their husbands jealous and stuff like that. I don't like to go out much."

"That doesn't sound very fun."

"And so that's why I'm single." He laughed, rather good-natured about it all. He sobered quickly. "Or was." He shot a quick glance her way.

"So women are nuts for bad-boy hockey players?" she asked, intrigued.

"Yeah, and how are you still single? Or were. Until me. With this. Now."

"Sweetheart Creek." Although for the number of football games she'd gone to with her matchmaking friend Jackie, it was a miracle she wasn't married eight times over.

"That makes no sense. The town is all about marriage. They still have that weird New Year's Eve tradition where you can elope if you go to that chapel on the hill like Brant and April did."

She gave him a dry look. The way their eyes locked sent a funny feeling down to her gut. "Eloping is ridiculous."

He chuckled at her frown. "I don't understand the blame you're laying on Sweetheart Creek for your single status. Doesn't the town have the state's youngest average marrying age or something like that?"

"The first seven-hundred generations stole all of my luck in that department."

But now she was in a relationship with Maverick Blades, which meant things were picking up. She could feel it coming her way with as much promise as their first kiss.

MAVERICK STOPPED his car in Daisy-Mae's driveway. She'd left the porch light on, and her fluffy white dog watched them from the front window of her living room. He wanted to keep driving, to let their first date spin into days rather than hours.

"What do you do with your dog when you're working in the city?" he asked, turning off his car.

"April takes her. Their puppy and Ella love to play. How are the renovations coming at your place?"

He sensed she didn't want their date to end, either. It had been a fun evening. He wasn't sure if it was the lack of pressure because this was part business or because she was a friend, but this had been his best date ever. It felt natural. Full of potential and like the dates he saw his friends having. Dates where easy companionship led to weddings.

"The renovations are too slow for my mom's tastes," he said, answering her question.

"I thought she had her own place?"

"She does. I was planning to do the work on the house over a few years. You know, have the place ready by the time I retire from the league."

"You're retiring soon?"

He shrugged. In professional sports your retirement could happen at any time.

"You'll retire to Sweetheart Creek?"

He nodded, and he could have sworn her shoulders dropped a notch as she relaxed.

"Why is your mom in a hurry?"

"I'm not sure. My best guess is that she thinks I'll get impatient and hire someone. I've done it before."

"What's wrong with that?"

"She said my places were impersonal and pretentious."

Daisy-Mae laughed, reclining against the headrest. She was comfortable with him, and that brought a surge of pleasure. He'd worried she might feel it was weird to date him after him being the "friend" for so many years.

"So your mom is doing it all?"

"She's taken over. She likes bossing me and a few contractors around."

"Do you mind?" Daisy-Mae shifted in the seat, facing him more fully. One long leg peeked out from the slit in her dress.

"No, but she's quite the taskmaster. I get this weird feeling in my stomach every time I pass a hardware store now. Like she's going to jump out and drag me inside and make me buy shower curtains and silicone, then watch YouTube videos on home repairs."

"Why's that? Experience?"

"I think most people call it trauma."

She laughed loud enough her dog started barking from inside the house.

"I heard your ranch is a woman-free zone." There was a teasing hint in her tone.

"It is," he said somberly.

"Why?"

"It's my escape from the world. My retreat." He shifted, unsure how to explain without insulting her. Especially since he could see her breaking his rule and coming over—welcomed, even. "It's not somewhere I take my dates."

"I see."

"Not that...well, friends can come over. It's just that I..." He couldn't find the right words to express that this was his retreat from the world. A safe place with no drama.

"It's a sanctuary?"

"When my mom isn't there handing me a hammer or an oil can, it is." He gave her a smile to show he didn't actually mind his mom giving him tasks. With her direction, the house was shaping up a lot faster than he'd anticipated. That and the eagerness of his teammates to come over and help. Somehow working on his place on their days off had become a thing. Maybe because his mom kept them all fed, and some players lived far away from their own families and his mom made them feel welcome.

"What happened to your beach house? I heard you sold it because you're broke." The cab of the car was dark, but the light from her porch caught the twinkle in her eyes even though her tone was soft, curious.

He let out a huff of amusement. "Yeah. And the police had to break up drug parties there, too." Her eyes widened, and he quickly spilled the truth in case she actually believed him and the stories. "No, none of that. The place was gorgeous, but it never really felt like home. I hired Katie Reiter-Leham—I believe she's a friend of your friend Mandy from Blueberry Springs?"

"Oh? That's so cool!"

"Yeah, so she was in town while her husband was doing something medical somewhere. I can't recall the details. Anyway, she took care of the decorating."

"But you didn't like it?"

He shrugged. "I didn't give her any direction. I was gone for playoffs and just wanted to have some bedding and dishes when I returned, you know? I gave her free rein. It was gorgeous, but it never felt like home."

"I guess that makes sense if she didn't know you, and you didn't give her any insights. I know Brant and April loved using it for their honeymoon."

"That's probably the only good memory. Some friends borrowed the house for a weekend, had a big party, police came, press came…"

"Tainted?"

"Yeah."

"What about your city apartment?"

"Sweetheart Creek has always felt like home. I like

seeing trees and wildlife outside my window. Think you'll stay?" he asked, curious if she'd soon be making the opposite move and head into the city he'd left.

It was her turn to shrug. "I don't know. I'm sure commuting will get old. Violet's talking about getting us a small apartment so we can crash there a few nights a week." She was staring out across her yard, off into the darkness. He would give anything to know her thoughts right now.

It made sense for them both to live in the city. And yet, here they were. Living just outside Sweetheart Creek.

"Some of my work I can do from home. But I need a desk."

"Yeah?" he perked up. "Need help finding one?"

"They're pricy! At least the ones I like."

"My mom keeps showing up with furniture. She might know where you can find something suitable."

"Would you mind asking her? I'd like something older and with personality."

"I can text her. She's a bit of a night owl." He waved his phone, pretty certain that texting your mom at the end of a date was a faux pas. Actually, things like that could be why he didn't get many second dates. He held up his phone. "If you don't mind?"

"No, of course. Please."

"I just thought it might be uncool to text my mom during our date."

Daisy-Mae giggled. "It's fine. Really." She rested a hand briefly over his wrist.

Maverick shot off a text, his mom getting back to him instantly.

"She wants to know what style of desk."

Daisy-Mae frowned. "I don't know."

Maverick thought back to what he'd seen in her house. "You sure you want a desk? I could see you more likely to curl up in an armchair with a laptop and a fuzzy blanket."

"That's not very professional."

"You're working from home."

"Yeah, but at a desk."

He glanced at his phone as another text came in. "My mom wants to know if you want to go shopping next weekend? And she wants me to come so you'll have a truck." He glanced at Daisy-Mae. "You can just borrow it."

Realizing his mom was playing wingman, and he'd just shot her down, he quickly amended his statement. "Actually, Sunday is our team's day off next week. I'll swing by and get you. You might need me if you buy something heavy. And maybe we can grab supper afterward."

Daisy-Mae smiled. "It's a date."

"A date with my mother in tow?" He winced, and Daisy-Mae laughed.

"I like that you and your mom are close."

"The supper idea included only you and me."

"Okay." She opened her car door, and he leapt out of his own side, suddenly nervous. He felt like he had a shot with Daisy-Mae, and he wanted to get it right. Every moment of it.

He escorted her up the steps where she paused under the porch light, unlocking her door. The barking stopped and snuffling sounds started instead.

Daisy-Mae turned back to Maverick. "I guess this is good night?"

Without another thought, he wrapped his arms around her waist, bringing her body tight to his. She felt even better than in his imagination.

"Good night," he said, his mouth inches from hers.

"Good night, Maverick."

Her gaze softened as he dipped his head. She

stretched her neck slightly, angling her mouth upward to connect with his.

He kissed her softly. Her lips were sweet with chocolate from her earlier mocha, and before he could let himself get lost in her, he ended the kiss, hoping he was leaving her wanting more. A lot more.

Because if nothing else, he was a horrible, despicable man for the way he loved every second of the heated electric touch of his best friend's ex's lips upon his own. If kissing Daisy-Mae was sinning, save him a seat in hell because he wanted to do this all day long for the rest of his life.

CHAPTER 5

$\mathcal{D}$ aisy-Mae stared at the poster of the Dragons
captain that had been hung in her new office,
along with several other star players and hockey mem-
orabilia. She hadn't been the one to decorate, and if she
had, she wouldn't have chosen that particular poster.

Maverick was smiling at her, gloved hands stacked
on top of his stick, his hair damp from practice. He was
staring right at her, and every time she looked up, her
heart skipped a beat.

And he had been placed straight across from her
desk.

She knew what it felt like to kiss those lips.

She knew what it felt like to be held by those powerful arms.

The idea of working from home was gaining in appeal—if only for its lack of distractions.

Her phone screen lit up with a text message from
Maverick's mom, firming up their plans for desk
hunting.

Was her Sunday supper date afterward with Maverick still on? She hadn't seen a single photo of them or
their Saturday night date on social media, and it had
been almost two days. Them dating was supposed to be

huge, wasn't it? What had happened to all of that interest from the initial photos?

What if their fake-real thing was already over and she was being added to The One-Date Wonder's list of women?

She steadied her breathing. Maverick wasn't going to toss her aside just because their first date hadn't gone viral. She could argue that they needed to keep trying, plead her case. Louis would agree. Although maybe not after seeing their dinner bill.

She held her phone, fingers hesitating over the keyboard. Sunday shopping. Maverick would be there, and Daisy-Mae would be hanging out with him and his mom. Like they were a real couple, a serious one. Not a publicity couple that were locked in something just for show.

The swirling in her head intensified. She could easily wind up in a repeat Myles situation with this fake-real relationship, where she was more emotionally invested than her boyfriend.

Setting down her phone, she walked across the room, considering what she could do about Maverick's poster. She tugged at its frame. It was screwed into the wall.

She sighed and surveyed her office. There was no way she was going to be able to concentrate in this office unless she turned her desk to face the corner.

Or just kept her head down and did her work.

She got back to it and a few hours later, there was a knock on her door. She'd closed it earlier, much too distracted by all the hotties and semi-famous people who traipsed past on their way to the conference room at the end of the hall. Agents, players, Miranda—the team's owner—even Violet sometimes. Everyone seemed to pass by her office.

"Come in," she called, her heart hiccuping as she spied Maverick looking at her from his poster.

"Hey, am I interrupting?" The door opened a crack and the real Maverick appeared. Her heart did another skip.

She shook her head and sucked in a breath, fearing he was coming to say he was pulling out of their fake-real relationship.

The One-Date Wonder strikes again.

He nudged the door the rest of the way open with his shoulder, revealing that he'd brought them each coffee. His expression suggested he was happy to see her and not about to dump her.

She relaxed, unsure if she should stay seated or come over for a hug. Was it too soon to expect something like that as a hello? She opted to stand and stretch and watch his cues.

The man needed a haircut, a wayward curl falling across his brow as he gave the door a gentle kick to close it behind him without spilling his precious caffeine cargo. She really hoped he was letting his hair grow as some sort of hockey superstition involving wins and losses during the season. She loved the slightly unkempt look he had going on.

"Not interrupting at all, especially if that second cup is for me." She reached across her desk, accepting the takeout cup. "Organizing princess costumes for men your size is not an easy task."

His eyes narrowed for a split second before he chuckled. "I thought it was *you* they wanted dressing up like a princess during the games?"

The PR team had been pretty set on painting the Zamboni like a castle and turning the game into some sort of fairy tale on ice. Shooting that idea down had landed her this job—thanks to the man in front of her.

But yes, the princess costume had been sized for her, not him.

"I outgrew the princess phase a long time ago," she said with a wave of her hand, taking her seat again.

"Says the woman with a glass case full of tiaras and crowns."

She laughed. It was true. She displayed her pageant wins. Some pageants didn't allow the winners to keep the bling as it was passed down to the next year's winner. But sometimes she got to keep it. And what was the point of bling if you didn't show it off a bit? Especially when you'd worked so hard for it.

"What are the twins going to do with a woman like you? I bet your no-nonsense, direct Texan approach melts their brains every time you speak to them." He sat in one of the ugly plastic chairs that had been tossed into her office like a second thought. He crossed an ankle over his knee, leaning back, and she realized she could have pressed them into a tradition of a hug and a kiss hello.

She needed to think faster if she wanted to enjoy all the benefits of having Maverick as her boyfriend.

"It's...*interesting* coordinating my plans with theirs." She lifted her cup, curious what he had ordered. The cup was from The Gingerbread Café and it smelled like their November special, a spiced latte. With oat milk? She took a sip. It was. "How'd you know I'm hooked on this?" She hadn't ordered it during their date.

He shrugged.

"Are you psychic?"

"I have friends in the right places."

"Well, tell them I also like diamonds, white gold, Italian leather, the color blue..."

"Noted or already known."

"So how was speaking to Violet? Did she squeal all

over you?" She smirked as he rolled his eyes, settling deeper into his chair.

"She was a little excited. You told her?"

"About us? Yeah." She took a sip of her drink to mask her smile. Violet had almost hit the roof with her enthusiasm when Daisy-Mae had told her they were dating. And naturally, being her best friend, Violet had noted the hesitation in some of her answers relating to how and when she'd been asked out. So now Vi knew the full story from crush to fake-real dating.

"Nice to know your friends approve."

"How about yours?" She was curious what his friends thought.

"Men don't really interfere in that kind of stuff."

"It's not interfering!"

"Okay, take that sort of interest."

"Much better."

Maverick frowned as he took in her office. He gestured at the hockey posters hanging to his right. "Didn't peg this as your style." He turned, looking at the wall behind him, and grinned at the poster of himself. He swiveled back to her, aiming a thumb over his shoulder. "Except for that. Want me to sign it?" He leaned forward as though searching for a marker on her desk.

"If it helps your ego. But I should tell you I plan to use it for practicing darts later."

"You kill me."

"Your eyes could serve as bullseye. Or…maybe something lower."

"You'd think I'd wronged you," he said in a playful, wounded tone. "Was our first date that bad?"

She moved to the chair beside him, tagging his shoulder with a gentle flick of her fingers, her gaze lingering on his biceps. My goodness. He was wearing a T-shirt today, and the sleeves stretched mighty tight across the bulge of muscles.

"Is the PR team satisfied we went out?"

"They may have mentioned the lack of attention we garnered."

"So they're still trying to marry you off?" she asked, sipping her drink. "Because I really can't see you getting married while you're in hockey."

"I'm only getting married if you say yes," he said with serious casualness, their eyes meeting over the white lids of their cups.

She lowered her cup and stared at him hard. He was joking, she reminded her fluttering heart. Joking.

He tipped back his head, breaking eye contact as he took a long sip of coffee. "I'm too busy for a major commitment like that. Women want their men to be around for stuff like marriage. And proper relationships." His eyes darted her way.

"Yeah."

He was staring at her and she felt a stab of self-consciousness. "What?"

He shook his head, his voice soft. "Nothing. It's just…you understand me in a way most people don't."

"I've known you forever. That's all."

"It's something more than that."

She studied her cup, trying to hide the thrill that he felt it too—that connection that was beyond plain old familiarity that made them click. It was something deeper and stronger. Something you couldn't create. It was just there. Always had been.

Maverick reached across the space between them and gently stroked her cheek with his thumb. "You'll always be my sunshine as long as I'm gazing into your gorgeous blue eyes. You could tell me I'm on death's door, and I'd still see nothing but sunshine."

He was so sincere, so bare and honest she wasn't sure what to do about the power of his words. It felt like more than a line. More than something a fake boyfriend would say to his fake girlfriend.

"Hey," he said softly, leaning on his armrest, angling himself over the edge of his chair toward her. "I know we're at work, but can I kiss you?"

Daisy-Mae nodded, and he shifted closer like he had all the time in the world. Anticipation built inside her like someone was shaking a full bottle of soda. And she was the soda. She forced herself to wait and not to launch herself at him.

His lips gently touched hers and she was pretty confident she wouldn't be concentrating on work in this office for the rest of the day. He kissed her slowly, deeply.

"You're so far out of my league," he murmured, leaning back.

Daisy-Mae took a better look at him. "Me?"

"You." He leaned over, giving her another kiss.

"I think it's the other way around."

He nuzzled her nose, a soft smile in place. "Maybe we can sort it out while we're on our second date?"

MAVERICK WANTED to stay in Daisy-Mae's office all day and kiss her. But he had to jump on a plane in an hour for tonight's game in St. Louis. He really didn't want to go. For the first time he saw a glimpse of what life could be like outside of the NHL.

He immediately shut those thoughts down. Daisy-Mae, for all her flirting and the wonderful moments they had together, had chosen to date him to help the team. And yes, she had suggested they do some real dating, but pro hockey ate up relationships, and he would be a fool to believe otherwise.

"Still on for supper after desk shopping on Sunday?"

he asked.

She nodded, and their second date was confirmed. Good. He needed more time with her. More of those kisses that felt real, and to prove to her that this wasn't just a publicity thing for him. Truthfully, he'd been worried when their first date hadn't blown up and trended, or whatever it was supposed to do, that she'd call his image recovery hopeless and quit. Or that she'd have time to think about the frequency in which he'd been recognized on their date—considerably more than usual—and decide that dating him wasn't the life she wanted.

"What's your biggest regret?" he asked her suddenly. Boy, he had game, didn't he? They'd just been kissing and now he was asking her about negative things she probably never wanted to think about.

"Not coming around that desk sooner," she said. The wicked glint in her gaze was too inviting.

"Next time," he promised, certain that there would be one. He leaned across the space between their chairs and kissed her again.

"What's your biggest regret?"

"Won't tell you." Man, he was bad at conversations. If you asked a question, expect to have it volleyed back at you.

"Why not?"

Because his biggest regret wasn't in real estate, missed investment opportunities, or hockey. It was the day he let Myles call dibs on her. They'd both been awed, practically falling all over themselves to speak to her. But since she'd gone to the same school as Myles, it felt natural for him to get dibs.

Stupid.

"Mav?" Her tone was soft.

"Not taking the shot when I should have."

"Oh."

"It's a metaphor." He shifted, realizing she could quickly pin him, have him confessing, and he didn't want to reveal his secret obsession yet. He didn't want her feeling even more obligation to date him or to get freaked out and call it all off. "Speaking of shots, since we didn't seem to go viral, I guess we need a plan so I don't find myself drugged by the PR team and wake up married to a lovely stranger in Vegas some weekend."

She sighed, her shoulders dropping dramatically. "Yeah."

"I'll admit I was a bit of a shot blocker."

"A shot blocker?"

"I need to get used to flaunting our relationship, let people photograph us and all of that. Although, it may never feel right encouraging it." His lungs restricted at the thought. Putting Daisy-Mae out there where she could get hurt, attacked, or publicly picked apart? It went against his every bone.

"So we need to draw more attention?"

"Yup."

"I have an idea."

"Yeah?" He hoped it had to do with kissing her again. A lot.

"How do you feel about a wardrobe makeover? You know, wearing something a bit different?"

The way she narrowed her eyes had him shaking his head and holding up his hands as though he needed to physically ward her off. "No. No way. No, no, no."

"What?" she asked innocently.

"A princess?"

"It would draw *a lot* of attention."

He tipped his head back and groaned. She would not stop busting him over that.

Truthfully, he hoped she never did.

"What if you did it for charity? Dak is working on that one for sick kids that Miranda started for the

77

team…" She lifted her brows, trying to entice him to cross-dress. Publicly.

"I had something else in mind."

"What's that?"

He shrugged, doubting his idea. The idea of hiring their own paparazzi—AKA the team photographer to shadow them again—felt icky when he considered saying it out loud.

She bounced in her seat, her eyes lighting up. "Do crazy stuff in public like kiss and—"

"No." He frowned. He wanted to keep their lives personal. At least the kisses. The hot ones. An innocent peck was probably okay.

"Or have this secret elopement—which, of course, will hit all the major news channels—after a big, public engagement where you post signs up around the arena asking me to marry you?"

Actually, that would draw some serious attention.

"Ha!" She pointed at him in delight. "You're considering that one! Keep it in your back pocket. I was also thinking we could sunbathe on a yacht wearing not much—if you know what I mean. Have a helicopter fly overhead…"

He was pretty sure that growling sound was coming from him. He could feel the structure of the cup in his grip giving way to the pressure of his closing fist. As evenly as he could muster, he said, "I was thinking we could rehire the team photographer."

She fake pouted. "But that other stuff would be so much fun, Mavvie."

"The photographer worked the first time. We could build on the initial photos."

"You're not going to propose in front of the entire rink?" She gave a dramatic sigh, and he realized, like a sucker, that he'd fallen right into reacting to her teasing.

Except now he couldn't get the vision of them sunbathing together out of his mind, or that she might be receptive to an engagement. Would she say yes to him? For all of their lives, just the two of them? Quiet times. Busy times. They'd be together. Nobody else. No more of this dating garbage. Just two happy people in love, holding hands through the ups and downs of life.

Wow, okay. He needed to get his brain checked. He was way ahead of things here.

"The calls about deals are still coming in, right?" She looked concerned enough that he wanted to lie to her.

He shook his head. "It's early days, of course."

"So we could try going a bit more bold? Bigger? Play it up on the weekend?"

He felt a smile lift his mood again. He loved she wasn't afraid of fame, of sharing him a little. Even though he'd much rather stay out of the limelight and spend all of that time with her instead. It made him think that maybe he could have it all—a relationship and hockey—if it was with someone like Daisy-Mae.

"If we do, it means no shying away from the cameras."

He sighed involuntarily. "All right."

"And I should know some things."

"Like what?"

"Like...what do you look for in a woman?"

"Why do you need to know that?"

"So I can be her. Make it believable."

"Never change for a man, Daisy-Mae."

She rolled her eyes. "It's not like that."

He stared at her, furious that she might think she had to change for him in order to be someone he wanted to be with. Obviously he wasn't very good at making himself clear.

He slammed his coffee down on her desk as he stood. He took her hand, pulled her to standing. She looked alarmed when he yanked the cup from her hand and set it beside his own. She was babbling something about judges and playing to their biases and that the public was similar.

He pulled her against him.

"Never ever change for me. Ever."

Her eyes were wide, and she went quiet. Then he gave her a kiss that would remove all doubt that she was the only woman he wanted—exactly the way she was.

———

BY THE TIME Maverick stopped kissing her she was dazed, her legs unsteady and her mind a shattered mess.

She felt disheveled and disoriented.

He released her, his eyes steady, locked on hers. Daisy-Mae was the first to look away as she sat back down again to give her legs a chance to recover.

What on earth was that?

That kiss. It was… She'd never been kissed like that. Ever.

She blinked up at him. He cleared his throat and retrieved their coffees. He held onto her cup until she met his gaze again. Then he gave her a slow smile so full of promises and heat it was all she could do not to grin like a fool.

She'd just had her brains kissed out. At work.

"So," she said, "don't change. Gotcha." Her voice was breathy, and she didn't know whether to go find a cold shower somewhere or straddle Maverick in his chair.

"So what I want? I want to be friends first. That's important to me." He was watching her, his cup cradled in his large hands.

"Okay." She thought about it. "We're friends, right?"

"We are."

"Okay. First check mark."

"I like smart women who are fun and easy to be around."

"Oh, I am checking off all of your boxes!" Her tone was light, but inside she felt like her very foundation had been rocked. She felt spooked. Maverick might like her as much as she did him. She might actually have a chance. And if she actually had a chance....

"Getting along with my family and friends is vital."

"Check. And I don't kick animals. I'm a nice person."

"Outspoken."

"Wait. I thought we were listing my qualities?"

He laughed. "You're the right kind of loudmouth. It's a list-worthy quality. Trust me."

What was there *not* to love about this man?

"A loudmouth for the greater good?" she teased.

"Something like that."

"And what does your dream woman dress like?" She dropped a touch of honey in her tone and he leaned in.

"Like you, I guess."

She loved the game where you played casual, and like you were unaffected by each other. You both acted like you were unbothered. Then when one of you finally broke, you had crazy-hot kisses.

Absolutely loved it.

"Which version? The before or after Daisy-Mae?"

"The one who wears my name and number on her back." He leaned close. "Not Leo's, or Landon's, or Dylan's. *Mine.*"

She was never getting that image out of her head of him wanting his name on her back.

"You're encouraging favoritism from the ticket holder experience manager?"

"It's called wearing your boyfriend's number," he growled. "It's a thing."

81

CHAPTER 6

Shopping was boring. Which was exactly why Maverick had hired out the decorating of his home so many times.

To make it more torturous, whenever it appeared Daisy-Mae had found a suitable desk and he'd offer to bring the truck around, it would send her and his mom into further fits of hemming and hawing.

He was pretty sure he'd seen every desk in every antique shop within sixty miles of Sweetheart Creek. And now they were in San Antonio, looking at office furniture so sleek and modern there was no way he could ever see Daisy-Mae using it. He was starting to believe they were messing with him.

"I think I like the one we saw in the first store," Daisy-Mae said thoughtfully, and Maverick held in a groan.

She burst into a sunny smile after a shared look with his mom, then gave him a playful nudge. "Just teasing! I'm buying Mrs. Fisher's old desk."

The third one they'd looked at. Because they hadn't just looked in stores today. Nope. They'd crawled the used ads online as well. In and out of houses all across the countryside.

"I'm going to check next door again," his mom said, zipping out the glass doors and back to the neighboring antique shop, leaving them to trail after her.

Unable to help himself, Maverick asked Daisy-Mae, "Then what was all of this about?" He gestured to the modern furniture behind them, then more generally, thinking of all the ground they'd covered.

"Mrs. Fisher told me to see if I found anything better, and then to let her know what a fair price would be if I still wanted hers by the end of the day. Now I know."

"So you didn't need me and didn't need my truck?"

She wrapped her arm around his waist as they reentered the antique shop, his mother already deep into the store. They stood near the entrance, waiting for her.

"Of course I needed you. What if I'd found something better and I needed to bring it home immediately?"

"I think we bored the photographer to tears," Maverick said, empathizing with the man who'd been shadowing them for the past several hours. He was leaning against an old bookcase, stifling a yawn.

"I suppose being domestic isn't very exciting."

Domestic.

A second date wasn't supposed to be domestic.

It was supposed to be as sexy as her outfit—tight jeans and an oversized Dragons jersey with his name and number printed on the back. That outfit had given him feelings. But not a single one of them could be described as domestic.

"Your mom?" Daisy-Mae whispered. "You haven't told her, have you?"

"She knows we're dating."

Daisy-Mae gave him a look. Why couldn't they just say they were dating? Why did they have to keep reminding each other that they had started seeing each other for a reason other than romance?

He gave a small shake of his head. He hadn't told his mom that a game was afoot. Because if Daisy-Mae fell in love with him, it wouldn't matter what had motivated them to go on their first few dates.

Daisy-Mae frowned. "Well, let's make sure she doesn't find out we're sort of lying to her. She looks really happy."

She did, too. She'd practically been floating through the stores, laughing, cheerful and full of energy.

"Maverick!" His mom beckoned to them from near the checkout counter along the left wall.

"I think she found something else for you," Daisy-Mae teased.

He rolled his eyes. The shopping trip for Daisy-Mae had been more fruitful for him with his mom collecting items for his house in nearly every store.

Maybe that was the real reason she was so happy. He'd let her decorate, and today he was present, weighing in on her ideas and decisions.

Why hadn't he made time to do this sooner? His mom had sacrificed a lot to ensure he got all the same hockey opportunities the other kids got, even though it was just the two of them. She'd taken extra shifts to get the right days off in order to take him to tournaments, driving late into the night or starting the day unreasonably early to save on hotel costs. His mom had been caffeine fueled most of his childhood, and how she'd pulled it all off, he still didn't know. She had lots of little tricks, like if she was baking muffins, she tripled the recipe and froze the extras. And she'd kept her hair super short in what he thought of as hockey mom hair so she could roll out of bed, quickly style her damp hair with her fingers on her way out the door at some ungodly hour, ensuring they made it to his team's scheduled ice time. His mom was his greatest supporter and always had been.

It had taken a lot of subterfuge and clandestine phone calls to pay off her mortgage for her as well as to get a plumber and electrician in to update her pipes and wiring—without her blocking him and refusing his help.

But his time and presence? That was what she really wanted. And it was the one thing he had in short supply but should never deny her.

"What did you find?" he asked, giving his mom's shoulder an affectionate squeeze as he came up alongside her.

She was beaming at a large dining room table. Wood. Old. Heavy. Stained sort of orangish-red. It looked almost as ancient as the state of Texas. He liked it.

"Would this fit in your truck?" she asked.

"I thought we weren't going to buy stuff for the living room and dining room until the floors are done."

She waved a hand. "The floor guy had a cancelation. He's sanding and refinishing it tomorrow."

"Tomorrow?"

"You'll need this for Friday." She flipped over the price tag, reading the item's history even though Maverick was certain she'd already committed it to memory. "We can put this in the barn until the floor is done."

"Why Friday?"

"Thanksgiving."

"Thanksgiving's on Thursday."

"How much to have it delivered?" she asked the salesman who was hovering, sensing a sale was about to be made.

"There's room in the truck."

"Then we'll take it," she said. "And the eight chairs, if they're included."

"They are."

"Excellent."

"What's Friday?" Maverick asked.

"We're doing Thanksgiving."

"We are?"

"Yes," she said firmly. She turned to Daisy-Mae, who'd been standing a few feet away. "Are you busy Friday?"

"No?" She looked at Maverick, and he hated she had to check in with him about family events. He wished it was assumed that she would be there, at his side.

"Of course she'll be there," he said. Catching himself, he added, "Won't you?"

"At your place?" she asked, again hesitating.

"Yeah." What was the holdup? Was she suddenly nervous about their masquerade in front of his mom? Was sharing holidays going too far?

His mom squeezed his arm. "Your woman-free zone?" She gave Maverick a pointed look like he'd wiped his nose with the back of his hand rather than used a tissue. Or forgotten to say thank you. Or, in this case, hadn't yet invited his girlfriend over to his house. His sanctuary. A place where he could be himself with no one there to muddy the waters and twist him into something he wasn't.

"It's Thanksgiving. It's an everyone zone," he said, hoping he didn't regret his words.

His mom smiled in approval. "Great. There will be nine of us, so we need to round up another chair. I think I saw one similar to these in that store back in..." She snapped her fingers, trying to recall. "Daisy-Mae, what was the store with that funny rooster statue Maverick hated?"

Daisy-Mae tossed out possibilities until his mom

nodded. "That's the place. There next. After we load up. Then we'll take this all back to Maverick's barn so we'll have room to go grab your desk." She patted the counter. "Pay the man, hon."

As Maverick opened his wallet, he figured he should be annoyed by the way his mom had taken over today, as well as invited Daisy-Mae into his woman-free zone. And yet, somehow, he couldn't quite seem to get there.

Same with his boredom. While he hadn't been interested in the items being considered in the various stores, he'd enjoyed watching his mom and Daisy-Mae connect and become what he thought of as friends.

He smiled as he took his receipt, not even minding that Daisy-Mae would be invading his home. In fact, he could already picture her working in one of the upstairs bedrooms on Mrs. Fisher's old desk. That was, if she didn't just curl up on a couch by the old brick fireplace in the living room. He'd have to make sure he bought a suitable couch for working on—not too soft. She'd definitely spend some time working there before they'd have to build an addition onto the house when they needed to turn her office into a nursery.

DAISY-MAE WAS NERVOUS.

She ran her hands down her skirt again before retrieving the cupcakes from the passenger seat. She noted the heaves and cracks in Maverick's front walk as she navigated her way closer to his woman-free zone. He wasn't that far outside Sweetheart Creek, and his hundred acres were off the beaten path enough that nobody had discovered him out here. His homestead was small by Texas standards, but she could tell by the way he talked that he liked it.

There was a modest barn behind the house where

they had unloaded his furniture purchases last Sunday and where he parked his Mustang. The old structure had been pressured by gravity for decades and had a slight lean to it, as though it may eventually decide to lie down for a rest if Maverick didn't do something about it. Beyond that was pasture and a small herd of cattle, which she knew was his. And in front of her was the cutest, shabbiest looking farmhouse she'd ever seen.

She stopped, taking in the house. On the weekend, they'd zipped past it in the truck and she hadn't had a chance to give it a proper assessment. It had a wide porch along the front, complete with a swing. The dusty windows had fake shutters with design cutouts that matched the gingerbread carvings at the roof's peak and the corners of the porch pillars. During its prime the home had probably graced the covers of magazines, and it warmed her heart to know that a man like Maverick had bought it and would restore it to its former glory.

The front door swung open, then the screen door, which twisted wildly as one of its hinges let go. Maverick grabbed the door before it fell, unhooking it so he could lean it against the home's faded yellow wall.

"I guess Mom's right—Dak and I should have fixed the screen door when we were fixing the main one."

"Your house is adorable," Daisy-Mae said, still taking it in. It needed paint and a little TLC, but she could see its potential and exactly why he'd bought it. She hadn't even stepped inside, and she was smitten. As neglected as this home was, it made her own look like an uninspired rectangle plunked down in the hot, dry scrubland.

She wanted to live here. Even though the screen door lacked the ability to keep out bugs and critters.

"Adorable. Just what every man wants to hear,"

Maverick said, coming to join her. "Whatever happened to calling homes manly or stately?"

She curled into his side, lifting her cheek for a kiss. "Are you going to keep it yellow? Because pink would be cute." She grinned up at him and he landed a light kiss on her lips, then quickly came back to land a second, slower, deeper one.

With a hand on her lower back, he gazed up at his house. "No pink."

She inhaled gleefully as her mind made a connection. "The cupcake cottage."

"Sorry?"

"The cupcake cottage." She peeled back the lid from the container in her arms. The pastel icing on her cupcakes matched the faded paint. The swirls she had decorated echoed the carvings on his house. "You live in a cupcake."

He snatched one, peeling its paper liner. "You copied my house. The cupcake came second, meaning my house is not a cupcake."

"Hey, these are for dessert. And anyway, doesn't Athena have y'all on sugar restriction?"

"Don't tell my mom. Or Louis. Or Athena." He took a giant bite out of the cupcake. His brows lifted in surprise and he let out a contented sound. "These are fantastic."

"I know." She put the lid back on the cupcakes and brushed a dab of frosting from his chin.

He edged closer, his feet bracketing hers. "Where else do I have some?"

"You're fine, cupcake stealer."

He took the last half of the cupcake and lifted it to his mouth, smearing the pale yellow and blue icing along his top lip. He leaned closer. "How about now?"

She laughed and darted away before he could get her sticky. "You're a disaster!" His hand snaked around

89

her waist, and she squealed and giggled as he drew her to his side. "You'll make me drop my cupcakes."

"When you two are done flirting"—Dylan O'Neill stood on the porch with his crutches, looking amused —"your mom wants to know if you fixed that last chair."

Maverick groaned and released Daisy-Mae. "I thought making it into the NHL would get her to ease up on the chores."

"I heard that," his mom, Carol, said from the doorway. "And the only way I'm letting up is when you get married and have somebody else nagging you to get these things done. There's more to life than hockey."

Maverick and Dylan laughed, knowing that when the team was in season, there really wasn't much more to life than hockey, as much as their families wished there was.

Dylan and Carol filtered back into the house with Maverick and Daisy-Mae trailing behind.

"And Maverick, wash your face," Carol scolded, popping her head through the doorway as they approached.

Maverick's tongue flicked at his lips guiltily as they stepped into the entry, and Daisy-Mae laughed. "You'd better wash up."

"Good idea." He tagged her lightly on the hip, pivoting into a room immediately to the right.

Daisy-Mae took in his house from the front door. It smelled like turkey, seasonings, and a home with history. The floors were wood, shining from their recent abuse with a sander and layers of new finish. The odd dark gouge or scratch showed through, proved their originality, giving the home character. The walls had the unevenness that spoke of lathe and plaster, and she could see some partially completed projects from where she stood.

To her right, the sound of running water trickled her way from where a small bathroom had been tucked. There was a short wall between the powder room doorway and a staircase leading up to the second floor. She stepped forward, checking her hair in the mirror above the small table Carol had picked up last weekend.

The house was smaller than she had expected but gave the illusion of being larger due to the sunshine streaming in from the living room just beyond the staircase.

Daisy-Mae set her purse on the table's lower braces, which had been made to also serve as a shelf. As she straightened with her cupcakes, her eyes caught on the items resting on the table. A wooden bowl with a few sets of car keys. Maverick's, no doubt. Beside that sat a small, clear stand-up frame meant for rare hockey cards. But inside was something homemade. Something familiar.

With her heart beating, she set down her container and picked up the case, staring at the card she'd created almost fifteen years ago. Maybe more.

An old, last-minute birthday present she'd made for Maverick. The hockey card was worn, tattered along the corners, and appeared as though it had been folded in half at one point.

She smiled at the details she'd put into the card. She'd cut out a candid photo of Maverick's face, gluing it on the two-and-a-half by three-and-a-half-inch piece of card stock. Then she'd drawn and colored in the rest of the hockey player's body. His name was written above with his old junior number, thirteen. Serendipitously, she'd colored his jersey gold, green, and black. The Dragons' colors.

She turned the case over, reading the back of the card. She'd listed his player stats such as his height, weight, position, and age, and then had made up further information. It was startlingly close to the truth. When she read the last line, she laughed out loud.

Maverick appeared beside her, his face freshly washed. "My mom found that in my things and had it framed. Crazy how close to true it is."

She showed him the back. "I was your agent!" She laughed again. "What was I thinking when I made this?"

His hands weaved their way around her waist, holding her close. "You'd make a great agent."

"Because I said princesses don't belong in the NHL and that you deserved better?"

"You protect my image better than my actual agent does sometimes, but that's not the reason I'm glad you're not my agent." He dropped a kiss on her nose.

"And why's that?"

"Because instead you get to be my girlfriend."

MAVERICK WAS BRINGING the fixed chair in from the barn when he overheard Violet say to Daisy-Mae, "I thought you two were trying to get more publicity around your *relationship*."

"We are," Daisy-Mae said, laying out the silverware. "It's just hard finding something genuine."

"Here's the chair," Maverick said, sliding it into place at the table the women were setting up for dinner.

Daisy-Mae gave him a weak, guilty smile and he gave a shrug to indicate he didn't mind them talking about the business side of their relationship—as long as his mom didn't overhear.

"You two need to do something big," Violet said. "Maverick, be a man and kiss the living daylights out of this woman on the Jumbotron." She gestured to Daisy-Mae, who blushed in her rosy pink sweater.

"I can see you're thinking about it!" Violet exclaimed. "Make sure you always keep your hair perfect," she said to Daisy-Mae. "Oh, who am I kidding? You're always perfect."

Maverick agreed. He also liked Violet's loyalty.

"Thanks for inviting us to your testosterone zone," Violet said.

Maverick rolled his eyes. He should have known better than to tell Myles and Dak that he didn't want women here. He would never live it down.

"You bet," he said.

Honestly, now that they were here, he realized how immature his proclamation had been. Friends—of any sex—made a house feel like a home.

"But I think it needs some womanly touches. What do you think?" Violet shifted a centerpiece left, then right. "It's a housewarming gift from me and Daisy-Mae. We found it at the church rummage sale and it just screamed 'Maverick.' We knew you had to have it."

He rolled his eyes. It was the ugliest fake floral arrangement he'd ever seen.

Violet giggled. "Just kidding." She took the basket of faded flowers and drop-kicked it into the living room, sending dust and petals flying. "Daisy-Mae found it on the back porch when we were feeding Milo."

"Who's—oh, Dak's dog? He can come in." He glanced around. "Where is Dak?"

"He and Dylan are chatting out in the yard," Daisy-Mae replied. She added in a whisper, "Jenny's out there, too. I think she has a crush on Dylan."

"Totally reciprocated," Violet chimed in.

Maverick's mom came through the kitchen doorway to check on the table. "It's looking good, ladies. Thank you." She frowned at the scattered flowers behind Violet. "Didn't we throw that out?"

"Milo found it," Daisy-Mae said.

"Oh."

"The bin," Maverick said, realizing why the arrangement had appeared slightly familiar. There was a massive bin for his renovation trash out front, as well as for the few household effects that had been left behind. How the dog had retrieved the arrangement was anyone's guess.

"I should schedule the truck to come empty it."

"I can do it if you give me the number."

"The floors look really good, Carol," Daisy-Mae said.

"They do, don't they?" She smiled.

Maverick still saw projects everywhere he looked, but the house was coming along quickly. "Thanks for arranging to have them done."

"I had an ulterior motive," she said with a wink.

"Why doesn't that surprise me?"

"You were using it as an excuse not to get furniture. I don't know how long you planned to live like a nomad." She turned to Daisy-Mae. "He was sleeping on a mattress tossed on the floor and living out of a suitcase."

"Really?" Daisy-Mae gave him a funny look.

"In the summer I planned to take care of some of this stuff."

"That's exactly what I was afraid of. You'd be exhausted from the season and hire it out again. I hope you're ready to keep this man in line, Daisy-Mae. Whenever he's given the chance he turns into a minimalist hermit or hires someone to make his place look as generic as a chain hotel." A timer in the kitchen went off, and his mom zipped back through the doorway.

"What's wrong with that?" Maverick asked as he and Daisy-Mae followed. She shrugged.

His mom pulled a steaming dish from the oven and answered, "You can afford to live in a place that feels and looks like a home. You didn't even have a shower curtain!"

"So?"

Daisy-Mae was watching the conversation unfold with interest.

"You were ruining your wooden baseboards with all the splashing!"

Daisy-Mae giggled, ducking from the room to answer Violet's call about which side the water glasses went on.

"You're embarrassing me, Mom," he said quietly. He knew he didn't need to impress Daisy-Mae, but that didn't mean the instinct wasn't still there.

His mom brushed off his comment. "Daisy-Mae needs to know what she's getting herself into."

"She's not getting into anything."

His mom whirled, eyebrows raised. "What does that mean? You're not serious about her? Because you look serious."

"I just... I uh..."

"Uh, what?"

Man, his mom had a way of nailing him to the wall, didn't she? He was head over heels for Daisy-Mae, but he wasn't about to admit that to his mother.

His mom turned back to the stove, stirring and poking at her various pots. "Did you plan to hold her at arm's length forever and never invite her over? You have to let women into your life, Maverick. Especially girlfriends. You shouldn't need your mother setting you up all the time."

"Hey, I asked her out, didn't I?" With some help from Louis.

His mom jammed her fists down on her hips, her eyes boring into him. "A woman like Daisy-Mae won't wait forever. She's looking for deep and forever, not some man who's never going to let her into his life and heart."

"I'm letting her in."

"Then why does she look like you're going to boot her out of here?"

"I'm not," he said with a laugh. "I like her being here, actually. Even though this *was* my woman-free zone."

"Oh, don't be so third grade." His mom pointed a wooden spoon at him. "She learned her lesson with Myles. She's not going to wait around until you figure out if you want her or not."

"So I should propose to her after dessert and scare her off?" he snapped, frustrated at his mom's pushing. He didn't want to ruin things with Daisy-Mae. She was too important.

"Don't be sassy. You know what I mean. Your career keeps you on the road and busy so much of the time. Make sure you show the woman you care about that she matters to you."

Maverick sighed. He understood what this was about now.

"She's not like Janie. She understands my schedule. She works for the team, remember?"

"Knowing and feeling are two different things. Let her know she's welcome here."

"She *is* welcome."

"She wants something real." She was eyeing him again. "And you need to figure out what you want."

Maverick muttered, "I know what I want."

He wasn't like Myles when, only a year ago, his friend had used him as a sounding board to help him figure out if Daisy-Mae was The One and if he should reignite things between them again.

If a woman was The One, you shouldn't have to ask a friend. You just knew.

And unlike Myles, he didn't have to ask anyone.

———————

DAISY-MAE HELD Maverick's hand as Leo, the team's rookie, said grace. Several players from the team had joined them for supper since they had played a Thanksgiving game last night and didn't have time to fly home to visit their families for the holiday.

This was Daisy-Mae's second meal since she'd spent last night with her parents, her father managing to get the day off for the first time in eons. More years than not, her mother's lack of interest in the holiday had sent Daisy-Mae to spend Thanksgiving at the Wylders' as an extension of their large family. This year, even though it felt slightly awkward being in Maverick's woman-free zone, she hoped this new NHL family filled the large Wylder family void.

To her right, at the head of the table, was Maverick. His mother, Carol, was at the opposite end. Violet was to Daisy-Mae's left, and Leo had grabbed a seat beside her. Across from Daisy-Mae was Dak, one of Maverick's old friends, who now worked with the Dragons Charity for Sick Kids. Beside him sat Jenny, a friend who owned the Blue Tumbleweed clothing store in town and who had been flirting and joking with Dylan, a player roughly the same age as Maverick, all evening.

As Leo finished saying grace, Daisy-Mae kept her eyes closed for an extra second, making a silent wish that her friends Jenny and Violet would soon find reciprocated true love. As she opened her eyes, she realized she probably should've made the wish for herself as well.

"Are we missing someone?" Daisy-Mae asked, referring to ninth chair which sat empty. Carol had insisted they buy it, and Maverick had fixed it as though it would be needed tonight. But there were only eight people at the table.

"You always want to have an extra chair," Carol said.

"It's a thing," Maverick mumbled to Daisy-Mae.

"A sign of a welcoming home," Carol said to Daisy-Mae as though this explained everything.

"It's for unexpected guests," Maverick whispered.

"Spirits?" Violet whispered loudly, leaning forward, her round eyes on Carol.

Jenny giggled and shook her head at Violet.

By the time dessert rolled around—pie and cupcakes—the table had gotten louder and louder with laughter and stories.

"You don't get dessert on your plan," Dylan said to Maverick, hobbling over in his air cast to swipe the cupcake off his plate.

"What?" Maverick looked so startled Daisy-Mae started laughing. Across from her, Dak joined in.

"You're almost as old as I am!" Maverick made a grab for the cupcake, but Dylan licked the top of it, claiming it.

"You're both too old to have dessert," Leo called out.

Dylan and Maverick, both close to aging out of the NHL, turned to him, their expressions dark.

Leo gripped the edge of the table as though preparing to run, his eyes wide.

"What was that, Socks?" Maverick asked, his voice low.

"You calling us old?" Dylan chimed in.

"Just sayin'..." Leo pushed his chair back a bit. "You know...with your broken foot and all... Rehab might be lengthy at your age and you might not—"

Dylan made a quick motion on his good foot as though he was going to lunge at Leo. The rookie jumped up so fast his chair tipped back and hit the floor.

The table erupted in laughter.

"I wasn't scared," Leo said, cautiously shuffling back to his seat again, trying not to smile.

"Sure, sure," Dylan said, taking his spot across from him while keeping a steady gaze on him.

"Socks?" Violet giggled. "Is that your team nickname? I had a cat named Socks."

"I had a mare with that name," Carol said calmly, obviously used to meal-time shenanigans—even at Thanksgiving.

"Can I have another?" Maverick asked Daisy-Mae, gesturing to the cupcake plate.

"Oops," Dak said, grabbing the last one as Daisy-Mae passed the plate. He took a giant bite.

"I used to call you a friend," Maverick said with a fake glower.

"You had one earlier, Maverick. Don't think we didn't notice," his mom said.

"Uh, how is your foot?" Leo asked Dylan as the man continued to glare at him from across the table.

"I'll hire the best when it's time to rehab. I'll pour my life into it."

"What I wouldn't do for a good deal and a pile of money in the bank," Leo said wistfully. "I've been chasing after Family Zone. I always envisioned representing them."

"They don't work with hockey players," Dak said.

"They should," Daisy-Mae said supportively. "They practically have their own team."

"Right?" Leo said. "And they're loaded. Theme parks, stores, teams, movies and TV. All kinds of crazy licensing and merch. I wish they wanted me."

Daisy-Mae met Maverick's eyes and he nodded slightly as though he, too, was wondering if they could somehow help Leo. She turned back to him, casually asking, "What do you need in order to get a deal with a company like that?"

"They want a family man. Squeaky clean. And I am!"

"You have a family?" Violet asked, her eyes dropping to his ring finger. Daisy-Mae noted the disappointment, even though his ring finger was bare.

"No, but he does a lot of squeaking," Maverick said with a smirk. Dak gave a snort of amused approval at the dig and held out his fist for a bump from his friend.

Daisy-Mae was learning quickly that the NHL was like its own family. With players often working far from home, they seemed to take each other in like brothers, looking out for each other, teasing each other, and sharing moments. As an only child, she loved it and wanted to be a part of it forever.

"I go to church, I volunteer," Leo said, ignoring the ribbing. "I'm helping with the team's charity for sick kids. I don't swear. I'm always polite and always helpful."

"You're a rookie," Maverick said gently.

"But I'm twenty-seven! I'm not even that young. I had deals on the bull riding circuit. Why not here, too?"

"You're young and unproven to these sponsors. They're waiting for you to go wild and crazy. You have time to earn your chops and get a big deal like Family Zone. Keep your eye on it and keep working them."

"I want this," Leo said, clenching his fork tightly.

"What's the rush?" Daisy-Mae asked.

"I want to make my money, and I want to get out. I want to raise a family, and actually be around for my kids." Leo's eyes met hers, bright and determined. He knew what his dream was, and he would get there. She knew that just by looking at him. "I want to be there when my kids take their first steps, when they say their first words. I don't want to be across the continent playing in a game and getting smashed into the boards, worried that I'm going to shatter my spine and not be able to do everything I want to with my family. There's a reason I left bull riding five years ago. Now I'm here, but I feel less in control of my future than when I was on top of bulls."

Daisy-Mae sighed. This man knew what he wanted. No conflicting reservations like she sometimes saw in Maverick. Then again, he was new to the team and didn't have the weight of the entire team resting on his shoulders. He could afford to be self-centered when it came to his career.

"Well," Daisy-Mae said after clearing her throat, noting that Violet was looking at Leo, slightly doe-eyed, "if there's anything I can do to help, let me know."

Maverick took her hand on top of the table and gave it a squeeze. Dak gave them a look of surprise.

His best pal. Maverick hadn't even told his best pal about them? They were supposed to be shouting it to the world through a megaphone.

Violet knew the full scoop and was rooting for them, but meanwhile Dak didn't even know Maverick was seeing someone—her. What did that mean? Was he trying to keep her in a work-only box? Don't tell your BFF, don't invite your gal into your woman-free zone?

"We'll think of something big," Daisy-Mae said, taking her hand back from Maverick's, feeling a tiny bit like she was getting in faster and deeper than Maverick was. She stood, starting to collect the dessert plates.

"Maverick, honey, can you start the coffee?" his mom asked. He stood and moved to the kitchen as Jenny and Dylan continued to tease and flirt at their end of the table. Carol asked hesitantly, "Are you two dating?"

Jenny said easily, "Sure, I'm his girlfriend. I have a

thing for hockey players." She rolled her eyes, but Daisy-Mae noticed that her cheeks had gone pink.

Dylan replied quickly, "I'm going to hold you to that."

Jenny shifted in her chair so she could face him more fully. "I'd like to see you try."

Daisy-Mae shot Maverick a look as they crossed paths in the kitchen doorway. Things were about to get fun. He took the pile of plates from her and she returned to her seat.

"I always need someone to be my plus one," Dylan was saying.

"Are you asking me if I'm interested in dating you?"

"Are you?"

"I don't know. Do you make the woman foot the bill?"

He looked offended, and Carol's eyes danced. She winked at Daisy-Mae as though she'd planned this, and Daisy-Mae grinned back. Maybe her earlier wish for her friends and their love lives would come true.

"How about holding the door open for me?" Jenny narrowed her eyes, assessing the built man sitting beside her. Dylan was a goofy, off-the-cuff kind of guy. Daisy-Mae would be surprised if anything came from this. Especially since Jenny rarely dated. But watching them spar and flirt was fun. It reminded her of the way she and Maverick verbally danced sometimes.

"Depends," Dylan replied. "Do you like it when men do that? Or do you find it annoying?"

"Annoying."

"Good. Then I won't. Unless you're wearing an impossible dress and need help to get out of the car."

"Do I look like I wear impossible dresses?"

"You own a clothing store. You might."

"She doesn't," Violet stated.

"And you drive a car?" Jenny asked. "Not a truck?"

"I do. Problem with that?"

"I don't know. Do you have a problem with the fact that *I* drive a truck?"

Maverick sucked in a breath as he sat again, no doubt very aware of the traps Jenny was laying at Dylan's feet. Daisy-Mae had a feeling Dylan could see them and was enjoying the challenge.

"My masculinity is safe and sound," Dylan said leaning back and crossing his arms. "So tell me more about how you go ga-ga for hockey stars?"

Beside her Maverick laughed, and Violet let out an "Oh, trouble!"

"Some star you are! You're benched, my friend." Leo winked at Jenny. "*I'm* a star though."

"One without a deal," she retorted, and Leo clutched his chest with a dramatic flourish. Dylan gave Leo a triumphant smirk.

"We'll get you a deal," Violet whispered supportively, rubbing his shoulder.

Jenny propped an elbow on the table, her brown hair cascading over her shoulders as she carefully watched Dylan. "I own my own business. I'm too busy to fawn over your stardom."

Dylan gave her a dazzling smile. "Yeah?"

Jenny sat back in her chair as though the conversation was over. "This was a very good meal, Carol. Thank you."

"You're welcome. I think you two have more to discuss. Have you been to that restaurant with all the hubcaps out on the highway. Myles loves it. What's it called Maverick?"

He shrugged.

"It's closed for renovations," Daisy-Mae said. "They had a flood."

"Well then—"

"Thanks, Carol," Dylan interrupted. "But I don't

think it would work out with Jenny. I like having a girl-friend who's around."

"I didn't say I wouldn't be around! I just happen to be busy too."

"Yes, very good supper," Violet said quickly, the rest of the table chiming in.

Jenny's cheeks were pink, and her hands were clutched into fists on the tabletop. "It's not about star-dom," Jenny said. "It's about time. *Making* time even if you're both busy. If you love someone and they're im-portant to you, you find the time."

"So wanna go on a date?" Dylan asked quietly.

At the end of the table, Carol's eyes danced and her chest expanded as she held her breath for Jenny's reply.

"Sure. Maybe. I don't know," Jenny said, clearly flus-tered. "Call me."

Daisy-Mae felt a warm hand squeeze hers. Mav-erick was watching her with a soft smile. He said qui-etly, "I'm glad we had the time for this supper tonight."

"Me, too."

He was a busy man with his career, commuting, renovating his house, and maintaining a close relation-ship with his mom. And yet he still found time to spend with her, to treat her right. And even though he was slow to allow her fully into his life, it was because he was careful with his trust. Being invited here along with a few of her friends to celebrate a holiday with him, his mom, and his friends was a big step. An im-portant one where they would begin to blend their lives.

It felt like he was not only inviting her into his life but also to become a part of his family.

CHAPTER 7

*M*averick took Daisy-Mae home after work, and as he dropped her off, he couldn't help but feel how wrong it was for them to be living apart. They'd been dating just shy of five weeks, but he wanted her to become a permanent fixture in his life. Even if it was too soon to think that way.

The sponsorship deals weren't rolling in for anyone on the team yet, his reputation had yet to be rewritten, and the publicity around them as a couple still remained pretty low-key as he did his best to avoid media frenzies. But he was happy, and he had a perfect excuse to spend time with his gal Daisy-Mae.

A timer flicked on Christmas lights that ran along the edge of her house as the sun set behind them.

"I like your lights," he said, drumming his fingers on the steering wheel. He didn't want to let her out of the vehicle, didn't want the evening to end. "Supper," he said in a fit of inspiration. "Have you had supper?"

"No. Have you?" She sounded amused.

He shook his head.

He was exhausted from commuting, practices, traveling for away games, and renovations. His life had become go, go, go, and he feared he wasn't showing

Daisy-Mae how important she was to him. Maybe that was part of why he wanted her in his home. It would be easier to hang out. They could go home together, enjoy a morning chat over coffee. Stealing minutes, making hours. Definitely easier than trying to navigate their schedules and separate households.

Yes, that was all. He wasn't in over his head with a woman who was dating him partly as a way to help others—and him.

Or at all paranoid about his mother's words about him not letting Daisy-Mae into his life enough so she'd know he cared as deeply as he did.

"Want to grab something at the Longhorn?"

"You can't eat there."

"Why? Because of Henry?"

She laughed. "No, because you're on a strict diet and the diner is all burgers and fries."

"They have that chicken wrap thing." They should have eaten in the city. He was going to have to make supper tonight, and he didn't enjoy cooking for one. So much work for a lonely meal.

"You've got to be getting tired of ordering that."

"It's okay, actually. But truthfully? I'm not sure I can handle listening to the diner's Christmas CD over and over again while we eat."

"I almost have the song order memorized."

"We should teach Mrs. Fisher how to use the shuffle button."

"Where's the fun in that?"

"Maybe we could fix her radio?"

"You're not a fan of Christmas music?"

He shrugged. "Maybe not listening to the same eight Country and Western Christmas songs over and over again. How about you? Do you get into the holiday? I like your lights."

She laughed. "You already said that." Daisy-Mae

pointed at the lights hung along her eaves with a sigh. "Don't ever leave them up all year though. They used to have color, but they're all faded now."

"I could help you. We could replace these with colored ones, and then I could help you take them down in January. Then back up again next winter."

"Nah, they still work—they're just not as colorful."

"But you bought colored lights," he pointed out.

"True."

"I don't have any decorations up at my place." In fact, he wasn't even sure if he had decorations any longer.

"You don't celebrate?" She tipped her head to the side.

"I do. I just…" He lifted his hands, giving her a helpless gesture.

She sighed in a way that reminded him of his mother. "Men," she muttered.

He chuckled. "What does that mean?"

"These things don't just happen, you know. You have to go out there and buy the tree. Kind of like if you want food in your fridge, you have to go to the grocery store."

"Now you're just busting my chops."

"I promised I would," she teased. She was relaxed, sitting back in her seat, obviously not eager to go back into her home and spend her evening alone, either. Even though she had her dog.

"Do you have a tree?"

"Yes. And I have food in my fridge."

"So do I. In fact," he said, an idea coming to him, "go get Ella."

"Why?"

"Get her. I have a plan."

"A plan?"

"I have something to prove to you."

She grinned, unbuckling her seatbelt and opening her door. "I like the sound of that. Back in a flash."

She hustled up the steps and, after what felt like forever, reappeared, small dog under her arm, a larger shoulder bag, and an entirely different outfit.

"Sorry," she said breathlessly as she climbed in. "Wardrobe change. Figured I didn't need work attire for you proving yourself to me."

"True." He patted Ella on the head and she sat, trembling with excitement on Daisy-Mae's lap, watching out the windshield as Maverick turned the truck around.

"Where are we going?" Daisy-Mae asked a few miles down the gravel road.

"My place. I'm making you supper."

"To prove you know where the grocery store is?"

"Something like that."

"Oh—turn here. She edged forward in her seat as they passed the turnoff for her friend Alexa, who owned Blueberry Creek Ranch.

"We're going to Alexa's?"

"Not quite." She began poking at her phone, then fiddling with his stereo.

Maverick went to protest, then realized he didn't mind if she played DJ or even paired her phone to his truck's stereo so she could use Bluetooth.

Soon Christmas music filled the cab.

"What's this?"

"We have to get you in the mood."

"That wasn't quite the kind of mood I was hoping to get into," he joked, giving her a wink. She blushed, and he knew that while he might have a crush on Daisy-Mae Ray, she had a crush right back.

"TURN IN HERE," Daisy-Mae commanded Maverick, pointing to a driveway that led off of the road to Alexa's ranch.

"Peppermint Lodge?" Maverick asked as they passed the lodge's sign at the turnoff.

Cassandra's Peppermint Lodge, a converted hunting lodge which shared the same road with her sister, was getting close. Cassandra moved here a year ago and this season had brought in some live Christmas trees. She was still deciding what to do with the lodge and its land and so far had been following the seasonal trends to bring in a little extra income for herself and her son. But Daisy-Mae knew what she truly wanted to do was create a wedding venue. It was just a problem of time and money to get it all going.

"Cassandra loves Christmas. And she has trees."

"For me?"

"Yes, but the best ones go first. Hopefully, she has something left."

"But it's barely December."

"Two weeks until Christmas, Mav."

"Where did November go?"

"You spent it chasing me." He'd been chasing up her free time whenever it coincided with his own. Dinner dates, coffee in her office, kisses after home games. So far they were doing pretty good with his insane schedule, although he'd had a string of away games last week, making it feel as though she'd barely seen him in the two weeks since Thanksgiving.

But she knew he was thinking of her. He'd call from airport lounges and had even sent her flowers once.

Daisy-Mae pointed to a spot near an old barn where Maverick could park. Strings of white lights, not faded like her Christmas lights, hung on posts around a corral with rows of trees waiting to be chosen.

"Good thing I drove my truck today," Maverick said.

Daisy-Mae took his hand outside the tree corral and Cassandra came out of the house in her boots and a flannel jacket.

"Hey, Daisy-Mae. Need a tree?"

"Maverick does."

"Wow, that's two NHL superstars buying trees from me now."

"You should put it in your advertising," Maverick said.

"Well, I'm sorta dating Landon. Does that count, or is it nepotism?"

"Pretty sure it is, but welcome to the world of business. Hey, how's Dusty doing?"

Cassandra's expression fell slightly, but she gave them a smile anyway. "He's doing okay. Thank you. He really loved having the team come to the hospital yesterday."

"He's still there?" Daisy-Mae asked.

"They're doing some tests and observations. He'll come home tomorrow."

"It was a lot of fun hanging out with the kids," Maverick said. "If he has ideas on more fun we can have, just let me know."

"Or Landon. Or me," Daisy-Mae added, feeling strangely possessive of Maverick. Maybe it was the way he was focusing on Cassandra, or the fact that Daisy-Mae knew he had a way of going more than the extra mile when it came to people in need. And Cassandra was a woman in need.

The conversation right now made her feel...well, she wasn't sure. But she'd probably choose insecure if she had to. Which was crazy because Landon, as much as the man hated to admit it, was head over heels for Cass. And Maverick looked at Daisy-Mae in a way that should remove all doubt that he liked her.

She supposed it was just the newness, the time

apart, and the fact that their relationship made the papers sometimes.

Although Maverick had also mentioned something about fearing that the public would criticize her and that dating him would make her a target. She knew, without him saying so, that it could twist back on him. All they had to do was say "former beauty queen" and there'd be a stigma that he was dating a bimbo, and poof! The image repairs would slide away.

Again, insecure. She knew it but sometimes felt powerless to pull up out of that nose dive.

"I heard about the fire in the hospital while the team was there," Daisy-Mae said. "I hope it didn't scare Dusty."

"Some wonderful photos came out of it," Cassandra said, smiling at Maverick. To Daisy-Mae she said, "These guys were carrying kids out!"

"We had to evacuate."

"Everyone was okay, though?" Daisy-Mae confirmed, even though she'd already seen the official report that a small fire had been confined to the hospital's cafeteria and that nobody had been hurt.

"Yeah, except maybe Jari." Maverick laughed and Daisy-Mae glanced at Cassandra, wondering who Jari was.

"Who's that?" Cassandra asked.

"Dak's ex. He owns The Gingerbread Café, and she showed up there afterward when we were all there." Maverick had texted Daisy-Mae to see if she wanted to meet them, but she'd been about to go into a meeting with a T-shirt distributor. "She tried to take on Miranda."

"The team's owner?" Cassandra asked. She let out a howl of amusement. "I bet that went well."

"It was a bit funny. If you were at a safe distance."

They stood awkwardly for a beat, then Cassandra

asked as she headed into the corral, "What size tree are you looking for?"

Soon they were putting a tree in the back of Maverick's truck and heading back to his place.

"Are you letting me into your woman-free zone again? Or will I have to wait in the truck?" She cuddled Ella closer. "Is that why you told me to bring her—for company?"

Maverick rolled his eyes and shook his head.

"No, wait! The real reason you didn't want women to come over was because your house looks like a cupcake! Sweet little cupcake cottage," she cooed. She deepened her voice. "So manly. Stately."

Maverick sighed and turned down his driveway.

"Come on, teasing is no fun if you clam up."

"You're never going to let me live it down, are you?"

"The cuteness of your house? Nope. Because I adore it."

"No, because I wanted a private sanctuary where nobody comes to party or comes by to drag my name and reputation through the mud."

"You're such a grumpy old man."

"I earned it."

She supposed that was true.

He parked his truck under the yard light, and they carted the tree into the living room, Ella dancing at their feet, barking with excitement.

"She loves real trees," Daisy-Mae said. They stopped moving once they got to the corner of the room and Maverick stood the tree up, holding it with one hand.

"You know what?" he said.

"I'm not sure I like the tone of that question…"

"I don't have a tree stand. At least I'm pretty sure I don't."

"How do you not know?" Men were such a mystery.

"I've moved a lot in the last few years, and people

112

were buying and selling off stuff for me. I don't know what I have anymore. Maybe my mom got one for me. She has a tab open at several places in town and is determined to have this place looking like a proper home before spring hits."

"Your credit card company must love you."

"I get a lot of points on my card, that's for sure. But to be honest, I appreciate what my mom's doing." He scrubbed a hand through his hair and took in his living room like he was just seeing it for the first time and wasn't sure what he thought of it. Then his eyes met Daisy-Mae's and his shoulders relaxed down a notch and he smiled.

"You know you're always welcome here. The no-zone doesn't apply to you."

All of her insecurities fled back to where they belonged in Stupidland.

He leaned the tree against the wall and pulled her into a hug, giving her a gentle kiss. "Now that I have you here, do you want to watch a movie? I'll let you lean against me. Maybe even give you a foot massage."

"A foot massage? It's a personal rule to never say no to that. Especially now that I'm wearing heels to work most days." She glanced around his living room. "You don't have a TV."

"Watch on my phone?"

A small screen would mean lots of cuddling. She liked that idea.

"Didn't you lure me here with the promise of supper?"

"I did." He dropped a kiss on the end of her nose and released her, heading toward the kitchen, Ella hot on his tail, her collar tag jingling.

As Daisy-Mae took in the sparse room she shook her head. Somehow Maverick always surprised her. They could go from domestic moments to fancy suppers to colleagues, and all of it felt natural. He was definitely a very special man who was stealing what was left of her not-so-available heart.

"HOW CAN I HELP?" Daisy-Mae scooted up to Maverick as he made supper. He was in the zone, moving around the kitchen, battering the basa fillets in egg and milk before dropping them into flour loaded with spices. Then into the pan with a touch of olive oil, the sound of sizzling filling the room.

"You can set the table." Timing was everything with fish, and he wanted dinner to be perfect for Daisy-Mae.

She opened the cupboard for the plates, already knowing where dishes were kept because of Thanksgiving.

"You have fancy plates," she noted.

"They've been in the family a while," he said from his station at the stove.

"And you use them every day?"

"Why not?" Why hold back using something you really enjoyed? Why save it?

"I don't know. I guess so they don't get broken?"

"Sure. That's a reason."

She set the table, and when she returned to the kitchen, Maverick handed her a plate of hot fish. He followed her out with a homemade spicy mayo from the fridge, having already prepped the mango, avocado, onion, and cilantro for the toppings. He set it all on the table along with a stack of whole wheat flatbread.

"This looks amazing," she said as they sat down across from each other.

"I hope I made enough."

She looked at the fillets and raised her brows. "I'm

pretty sure this is more than enough unless you still eat like you did as a teenager."

"I do."

Daisy-Mae followed Maverick's moves, building her own taco. He could see from her expression that she wasn't so sure about mango on top of fish. But upon her first bite, she closed her eyes, savoring the flavors. When she opened them again, Maverick smiled.

"You like it?"

"You're going to be sorry."

"Why's that?"

"I'm going to be over here mooching dinner all the time," she threatened.

His heart swelled at the thought. "Works for me." He took a large bite of his own taco, pleased with his cooking skills. He'd have to remember to thank his mom later.

"Do you always cook for yourself?" she asked when they were working on second helpings.

"Pretty much. Athena gives us a strict diet to follow during the season. It's easiest to just make the recipes she gives us."

"Is this one of hers?"

Maverick nodded.

"It's delicious. I should ask her for some recipes."

"What?" He tossed his hands upward as though bothered. "Now mooching off of me isn't good enough? You've got to go to the source?"

She giggled, giving him the sweetest smile. He could get used to this. Having her in his life, doing the things most couples took for granted.

When they had eaten their fill, they began packing up the leftovers. He'd definitely over-estimated how much Daisy-Mae would eat.

"I'm going to make myself a fish sandwich for to-morrow. You want one?"

"Cold fish?" Her mouth wrinkled into a frown.

"You don't trust me?"

"Okay, fine. But if it's gross, I'm going to march down to the rink and find you."

"Promises, promises."

He began prepping their sandwiches for the next day, a tidbit somehow falling from his steady hand and landing exactly in Ella's mouth.

"Oops." He gave Daisy-Mae an innocent look.

She laughed. "She's already got a huge crush on you, but I think that sealed her undying devotion."

Now he just had to figure out how to do the same with Ella's owner.

He finished the sandwiches, packing the fish separately. "Don't add the fish until right before you eat or everything'll get soggy." He set their lunches in the fridge, washed his hands, and checked his phone. "My mom says I have decorations in the barn."

He was barely finished the sentence before Daisy-Mae was moving to the front entry. "Let's go find them. I love decorating Christmas trees."

"Wait! We need a flashlight." He grumbled about her impatience as he moved past her, finding the large light he kept at the door.

He discovered he didn't mind the small entryway though. Moving around Daisy-Mae often caused her to place her hands on his waist, back, hip, or arm. He liked it. Too bad he couldn't think of more reasons to spend time in there.

In the barn, Maverick swung the flashlight left and right along the ground so they wouldn't trip on the boards, cables, spare parts, and other things left behind by the previous owners.

"Careful," he said, directing her around some metal pipe.

"You don't have lights in here?" Daisy-Mae asked.

"There's something wrong with the wiring. It's way down near the bottom of the to-do list somewhere."

He shone his flashlight past his car and toward a stack of boxes at the back of the small barn as they made their way closer to them.

"How's the herd doing, Mr. Cowboy?" she asked, giving the punching bag he'd hung from a rafter a delicate right jab.

"Gotta earn my hat and buckle," he joked.

"Why do you have cows? You're barely around."

"My hired hand takes good care of them when I can't get out there. Having my own herd is something I've always wanted. When I retire I plan to be more involved."

It still surprised him how much he wanted to prove his worth and belonging when it came to his land. He wanted the respect of the neighboring cowboys. And yet he didn't care that half the world thought he'd cheated with his ex-coach's wife and, as a result, would never respect him.

Although, to be fair, when he allowed himself to think about it, he did care what everyone thought about his bad boy reputation. The fact that there was a crowd of folks out there who believed he lacked integrity kept him up at night—especially when he thought about how it all reflected back on his mom and the work she'd put into raising him.

All because of one story. That one false story.

So, he did care. A lot more than he wanted to admit, in fact.

As they shuffled through the boxes, Daisy-Mae let out a soft gasp. Maverick was at her side in a flash.

"What's wrong?"

"Kittens!"

"Well, will you look at that?" he said, leaning to look past her. A litter of five kittens tottering around their

117

gray mother. "I've always wanted cats. We couldn't when I was a kid."

"Your mom's allergic?"

"No, we just couldn't afford it. But I can now."

"So much for your woman-free zone."

He realized that when it came to that rule, there was a lot of room for exceptions.

BACK IN THE house with the Christmas decorations, Maverick cracked an egg into a pan and began frying it.

Daisy-Mae, who'd been poking through the box in the living room, peeked her head into the kitchen. "Are you already hungry again?"

"It's for the cat," he said, knowing that he wouldn't be able to put his heart into decorating for Christmas until he'd taken care of the mama. "You can see her ribs." Her kittens seemed healthy enough, but they looked to be a few weeks old and were no doubt draining the mama cat's limited reserves.

Daisy-Mae wrapped her arms around his waist, and rested her cheek against the back of his shoulder blades. "That's sweet."

"She's hungry."

"You know she'll never leave if you feed her."

"Kind of like you?" he asked with a smile.

She let out a giggle. "Yeah, kind of like me."

His mom didn't know what she was talking about. Daisy-Mae knew how much he adored her and that she was always welcome here.

"For the record, I'm okay with all of that." He slid the cooked egg onto a plate, the scent of butter filling the air. "Besides, I could use a good mouser."

"How about six of them?"

He turned in Daisy-Mae's embrace, facing her.

118

"Once she's done nursing I'll have Brant spay her to help control the population. Then bring the kittens in once they're old enough, so they don't reproduce as well."

"You're going to keep them all?"

"If they want to stay, they're welcome. Can you grab me a bowl?"

While she got one, he chopped the egg into bite-size pieces, then went to the fridge for some of the fish leftovers. He took a small chunk from one of the fillets packed for his lunch, scraped off the spicy batter, and added it to the plate.

He took the bowl from Daisy-Mae and filled it with water, making sure it was cold and fresh. There was a small pond out back, but the mama cat shouldn't have to make the trek, deal with the mud, or the fact that the water was less than desirable.

He lifted the bowl and plate, blowing on the still-steaming egg.

"The cat chose the right barn," Daisy-Mae said.

"I'll be back in a minute to help decorate."

"You're taking the good dishes out there?"

He glanced at the meal he'd created. "Yeah?"

Daisy-Mae made a clucking sound that made him smile. She dug through the recycle bin by the back door that led off the small laundry room attached to the kitchen. She returned with two empty plastic containers. "Here. You'll get in less trouble from your mom this way."

That was a good point.

"Thanks."

Daisy-Mae was watching him with a warm expression. She stepped forward, brushing his cheek before planting a kiss on it. He had a feeling that just by being himself, he was winning some serious brownie points.

He loved that about Daisy-Mae. It was all so perfect, so easy.

"I'll be right back."

Maverick left the food and water a few feet from where the cat and her litter were stationed, afraid to disturb her by getting too close. He didn't want to spook her or make her feel she had to move her kittens elsewhere to keep them safe.

He headed back to the house, smiling at the light shining from the windows and the fact that there was a woman inside, waiting to decorate a Christmas tree with him.

Life was looking pretty good for this old defenseman, and the only way he could think to improve it would be to ask Daisy-Mae to be his wife.

CHAPTER 8

$\mathscr{I}$t was Wednesday night, and Maverick had just finished a home game. The Dragons' second win of the season—and long overdue. The team, from what Daisy-Mae had heard, was beginning to believe in curses.

And to make tonight's win even sweeter, Maverick had scored the winning goal against the team that had tossed him aside—Lafayette.

Daisy-Mae had wanted to dance, and as the mascot handler, she had. All over the arena, getting the fans worked into a frenzy of excitement for their home team. Her enthusiasm had been contagious, and she'd never felt an energy like that before. It made her want to become a performer.

Daisy-Mae, still in her Dragons puck bunny outfit, left Violet to finish primping her hair after being in the costume and went to wait outside the team's locker room for Maverick. He had to be crazy excited. The team, too.

The door opened, and he was the first one out, his hair damp from what must have been a quick shower. His jeans and light sweater clung to his muscles, and when he saw her his eyes lit up as he grinned.

"Hey, champ," she said, rolling up onto the toes of her boots to give him a kiss right on the lips in front of everyone. He dropped his duffle bag and hugged and kissed her back.

They got a few catcalls as other men entered the hallway, and Maverick scowled at them, making Daisy-Mae laugh.

"I saw you in the stands," he said, releasing her.

"Wow, you can focus on me *and* on making goals?"

"No. Not at all," he admitted. "Sometimes I sit on the bench, though, you know."

"Aren't you supposed to watch the ice when you're on the bench?"

"I told you back in October that you're a mighty distraction." He hefted his bag again, slinging its strap over his shoulder. "You're probably the reason we lose so often."

She gave a choked laugh. "The only wins this season have been when I'm up in the stands, buster."

He smirked and kissed her again.

"So? Where are we going to celebrate?" She was practically vibrating with energy from the win. And she was just the mascot's helper. She hadn't actually been on the ice. He must feel so full of energy, too.

"Celebrate?"

"Yes! Don't you feel good?" She ran her hands down his chest, then gripped his waist and pulled him closer.

He smiled. "Yeah. I feel pretty good."

Understated as always. She could see the joy lifting him like the earth's gravity had been reduced around him.

"You should feel amazing! And we need to be seen. We need to show you off because you just scored the winning goal against your old team." Daisy-Mae snuggled against him and patted his chest with pride.

"Can't we stay in?"

"Again?" Decorating the tree had been lovely last night, and she'd love to repeat having him all to herself, but they had a job to do. She'd noticed that sometimes after people recognized him, they grew cool, and she wanted to change that. She wanted the world to celebrate the Maverick she knew and adored.

She nudged him. "We're supposed to be out in the world, spreading this amazingness and making people love you again." She began pulling his hands, dragging him toward a cluster of teammates at the end of the hallway, just before the doors that would lead them to the press.

He resisted.

"What?" Didn't he see this opportunity to change the way people saw him? Or was something else happening that she hadn't picked up on yet?

"Can't we? You know?" He was eyeing the group of men. He looked back at her. "Just you and me? Do something away from everyone else?"

"You don't want to be seen with me?" Her words barely came out above a whisper as she caught herself. He was simply more private than many of his teammates and had been burned by the press. It wasn't about her. "I mean, we *have* to go out. We *have* to celebrate."

That lift she'd seen earlier seemed to fade.

"Let everyone celebrate you, Mav." Then she leaned in, her hair brushing his neck as she whispered a reminder. "It's part of the deal, right?"

She watched his expression, getting the feeling that he was really starting to hate that part of their relationship.

DAISY-MAE DIDN'T KNOW what to think. She'd practically had to strong-arm Maverick into celebrating his own win. And then once they were out, he kept hiding away, refusing to pose for the cameras with her. The photos that had been released didn't exactly exude love.

She didn't get it. He smiled that special smile for her, was always dropping by her office when he was in the city, stealing kisses here and there, phoning her when he was traveling.

It no longer made any sense.

It had been several days since the win—the last time they'd seen each other—and now he'd asked her to meet him for coffee.

Something had shifted between them, and she wasn't sure what it was. It felt like they were getting closer as a couple, but he was acting strangely, pulling back whenever they had a public commitment. Had she done something wrong? Was he afraid she was going to make him look bad?

It didn't help that Louis had called her into his office two days ago, looking tired and asking for the scoop.

There was no scoop.

Maybe Maverick was getting pressured by Louis, too, and it was making him seize up in public. He'd said he'd try to get better at the publicity stuff, but it felt like he was getting worse.

Leo and Landon still didn't have deals, and there were only four more months in the season since it would take a miracle to make playoffs, which would have extended their season by another two months and into June.

She slipped into the Longhorn Diner, scanning the room, which was decked out for Christmas.

She took a stool at the back, planning to order a coffee while she waited for Maverick.

"Hey, Levi," she said, recognizing the man one stool down. Cowboy hat, dark hair, blue eyes. Wylder through and through. She unwound the scarf his sister-in-law April had knitted her last year and bunched it on the counter.

"Hey, how's life?" he asked. "I barely see y'all these days."

"Yeah, life's kind of gotten busy," she said, shaking out her hair.

"Who's that gorgeous woman sitting alone?" Maverick said moments after she'd gotten herself settled.

"It's like he doesn't even see me when you're around," Levi joked, grinning at Maverick, who gave him a nod.

"Hey, stranger." Daisy-Mae slid off her stool to give Maverick a hug. He responded by pulling her into his arms, giving her an extra squeeze, and landing a kiss on her lips.

It made her believe everything was perfect—as well as wonder why he couldn't do this when the cameras were on them.

"Get a room," Mrs. Fisher, the ancient waitress, told them from behind the counter. She waved her coffeepot at them and they nodded.

Levi reached over the counter, grabbing Daisy-Mae and Maverick fresh cups for Mrs. Fisher to fill.

"Thanks, hon," she said, not even scolding him like usual for doing her job.

Maverick stole another quick kiss from Daisy-Mae as Mrs. Fisher filled the cups.

"You'll turn off the customers with all that smoochin'," Henry Wylder replied as he took a stool a few down from where they were standing. He jabbed a thumb toward his own chest. "*Me.*"

"We'll be over here, Mrs. Fisher," Daisy-Mae said, picking up the cups and gesturing at an empty booth.

"Want to order a bite?"

They shook their heads and made their way over to the booth.

"Is he still glaring at us?" Maverick whispered as they left the counter.

"Henry always glares at me."

"He's as ornery as Bill," Maverick muttered, referring to the armadillo that terrorized the town.

"Did you notice they added him to the welcome sign?" she asked, sliding into the booth.

"Henry? Please, no."

Daisy-Mae laughed. "One way to prevent the town from growing. But I meant Bill."

Maverick pushed his cup of coffee to the side after taking a sip, then reached across the table, sliding her hand into his. "I missed you on the weekend."

"I missed you, too. How was the game in South Carolina?"

"We won."

"I heard. You're on a streak."

"I'm the luckiest man."

"Finally, some good things are happening, right?"

"We even have some fans now." He winked at her good-naturedly. "The pyrotechnics from the home game the other night were a hit. Everyone's talking about the stuff you're doing."

She shrugged. "Anyone could have thought of that."

"But they didn't. It was like a rock concert within a sporting event, with parties in the parking lot like it was football before and after the game. Everyone wants Dragons gear."

She brushed off the compliment. "Miranda's getting slaughtered for the cost."

"By the suits in accounting?"

"The press."

"They just enjoy gunning for her."

"They think she's trying to buy team loyalty."

"So?"

They chuckled.

"I'm glad you got that job," Maverick said softly. "It's fun out there again. And our fans are enjoying it, too."

"That's just the wins talking."

"It's not."

"It's weird. The press really hasn't been talking about us at all. I thought we'd be getting somewhere by now."

"You crave the infamy of dating me?"

"Yeah," she said dryly. "I should have a medal for each date I successfully wrangle you into, shouldn't I? How is that not noteworthy?"

"I meant to ask," Maverick said, letting go of her hands and fidgeting with his coffee cup. "Do you want to go to the gala with me?"

"On Friday?" The team's charity was holding a fancy fundraiser. Very black tie. She, along with most staff, was going. Although it was unlikely she'd be able to afford to bid on a single thing at the silent auction. "I'd love to."

"I'll pick you up."

"I'm going to have to bring everything into work. I don't have time to come home afterward."

"Then I'll pick you up from there. Did you get an invitation to Myles and Karen's wedding?"

She nodded.

"Are you going?"

It was in February, on Valentine's Day. And while she wanted to ask Maverick to be her date more than anything, it was further into the future than the time they'd spent dating so far.

"I keep hoping something'll come up so I won't have

to go." She scrunched her nose. "Does that make me a bad person?"

"What if you went with me?"

She inhaled, wanting to say yes, but afraid she'd end up going solo and staring at two exes that night.

"Come on, don't break my average now. I've got an impressive track record of you saying yes to my dates."

DAISY-MAE WASN'T GIVING him an answer about being his wedding date.

"What? You don't want to go at all? Even with me?" Maverick asked, trying to sort out where her thoughts were.

"It's two months away. Will we still be together?"

Her words hit him hard in the chest. "Are you planning to break up with me before then?" He hadn't even considered that as a possible option.

"This fake thing isn't really helping you or the team, so I understand if you wanted to..." She shrank in her seat, giving him a cute I-don't-know look.

Seriously?

He thought they'd been making progress, and that she knew how committed he was.

He leaned forward, tamping down his frustration. He stroked her knuckles as he carefully chose his words. "We're doing okay, aren't we? Even though nobody's gossiping about us?"

"I think so." Her voice caught in her throat, and if it had been anyone else, he would have thought she was worried about being rejected or dumped. But this was Daisy-Mae, superwoman.

"Then it's settled. There are no plans to break up on the horizon, so you'll come as my date?" Maverick confirmed.

She gave a small nod.

Good. Nobody should go to their ex's wedding alone.

"Wait. I have a condition."

"Oh?"

"Will you wear a tie that matches my dress?"

"Sure."

She gave him an evil look. "Even if it's pink?"

"Even if it's pink."

"It won't be pink." She was studying him, and he had a feeling she was deciding what color they would wear.

He was good with whatever she wanted, but right now he had another question to ask.

"Do you want to come over for Christmas dinner?"

She blinked and stared at him.

"Come on, Daisy-Mae. I've got a great streak going here. Let me have the hat trick. Three yeses…" He was teasing, cajoling, and a tiny bit worried she was trying to find the publicity angle when he just wanted to call her a part of his family.

"Of course, yes, you silly goose."

Three big dates. This was turning into a good coffee.

He had one more thing, though…

"You're worried about our lack of publicity," he stated.

"Well, it was part of the deal," she said, taking her cup and winding her fingers around its smooth surface. "Louis was asking me about our plans."

"The press hasn't been as bloodthirsty lately." Dating Daisy-Mae did seem to be quietly helping, even though there wasn't any big fanfare about them.

"I've noticed."

"Thanks for your help with that."

She smiled. "It's been my pleasure." Her cheeks flushed slightly. "But we haven't really been maximizing our opportunities. I know you're not exactly an attention hound, but maybe there's something we can do to give things a small kick."

He narrowed in on her words, the opportunity that was coming his way.

"You want to maximize things?" he asked.

"I think we should."

He leaned forward again. "How about this? If nothing moves the needle on my reputation or deals for Landon and Leo by New Year's Eve…" He paused. Was he really going to put this out there? Take a risk and ratchet up the fake angle when all he wanted was real when it came to Daisy-Mae?

Yeah, yeah, he was willing to take that risk in hopes of winning all of her.

"What?" she asked, leaning closer, her gaze on his lips.

He swallowed hard, trying to will his voice to sound casual as he said, "I'll propose to you. Publicly."

PROPOSE.

That meant engaged.

She'd be engaged to Maverick Blades.

He'd be hers. His heart, his time and attention.

But they'd be faking their level of commitment, wouldn't they?

Although, a fake engagement where she had to kiss those frowning lips and have him light up when he saw her? Amazing idea. Even better than dating.

It would be a job. A duty.

But it was Maverick, and every moment with him felt like sunshine on her soul.

She held onto the beginnings of a smile.

It faded. It would suck when he broke up with her.

She could only imagine her mother's words about what a fool she'd been. Not only would Daisy-Mae carry the stigma of being a former beauty queen, but also the ex-fiancée of an NHL star. A star who didn't date anyone more than once. And who had all but welcomed her into his woman-free zone—like she didn't count?

No. She needed to clear her mind and focus on what she felt—what was real. She was already falling in love.

But it wasn't a guarantee that he'd be falling, too. He was suggesting an engagement as a publicity stunt.

Daisy-Mae, say hello to a total Myles repeat.

Maverick reached across the table, his expression growing more and more worried as the seconds ticked by and she remained silent.

Being engaged to Maverick would be amazing. She was sure of it. He was sweet. And fun and easy to be with. He was a rock of muscle. Hot. Strong. Safe.

"I don't think we're quite there in our relationship," she said, wincing. This wasn't about their relationship or how either of them felt. They were real dating, but an engagement this soon wouldn't be.

And possibly, it could ruin everything.

She really wanted it, though. But what could she do? Admit this had become very personal to her and she'd only ever say yes out of love?

"Yeah, it's for a pop of publicity," he said quickly, his Adam's apple bobbing.

"If we get engaged and then break up, it'll backfire. We'll look stupid. Engagements are for people in love. Doing it for public approval is taking things too far."

"Daisy-Mae, I don't know if you know this, but I'm kind of falling for you over here."

She laughed.

"No. I'm serious."

She met his solid gaze and realized it was true.

131

Maverick hadn't led with it, but he had feelings. Serious, true feelings for her.

"It could help, but it's a lie," she said tentatively, hoping he'd correct her and confirm that this might be love for him, too.

"Maybe it's not a lie."

Her heart lifted like it was going to explode out of the top of her chest.

Maverick Blades.

This might shape up to become the best day of her life so far. She leaned over the table, kissing him firmly.

"I know it's early," he said when she stopped kissing him, "but maybe one day you might also––"

"Maverick Blades, you silly, dense man," she snapped before she could stop herself. "I have been crushing on you for so many years. And dating you has only made those feelings stronger. I love the way you treat me, and you have been the best boyfriend. Ever."

She waited for that to sink in.

He tipped his head slightly. "Ever?"

"I'm just sorry it's taken us so long to get here." She gave him another kiss, and Mrs. Fisher, who'd come by to give their cups a top up, quickly kept going.

"Well, I don't know about you, but I want to move fast."

She thought about it for a moment. They'd known each other as friends for a long time, so maybe this wasn't so crazy after all. Maybe it wasn't such a huge blur or a rush.

"I'll let you think on the plan for the New Year, but just assume you're going everywhere as my date from here on out, okay?"

She stuck out her hand, shaking his, unable to block her giant grin. "Deal."

He gave her a funny look as she released his hand.

"Sorry. I might be a tad excited."

"I think I finally understand why Myles and Karen got so deep, so fast."

"Because when you're as old as we are—"

"And been around the dating track so many times—"

"You just know."

"You just know," he echoed.

They shared a smile.

"So when are you moving in with me?" he asked.

She laughed, and he joined in.

"Too fast?"

"Just a tiny bit."

"I want to go fast, but I also want to get this right. I don't wanna skip any of the important steps."

She nodded, understanding.

"We'll have a long engagement then," she said. She thought about it for a second. "Longish." Not too long.

"And you and I?" he asked.

"We're real. Nothing fake between us any longer," she said softly. Not even a possible engagement.

"And we go at your pace."

"Then you'd better go ring shopping."

133

CHAPTER 9

*M*averick couldn't believe how well that coffee date had gone. Daisy-Mae was in love with him. He felt like singing, clicking his heels, whistling, and throwing money from the sky.

She'd told him to go buy a ring.

He was so glad he hadn't waited until he was retired to try his luck in the love department again. He'd found the right woman for him, and she'd been there the whole time. He shouldn't have postponed things for so long. They'd missed so much time they could have spent together.

Sure, part of the engagement was for spectacle, but if their crazy idea worked, not only would he soon be married to Daisy-Mae, he might also swing some nice deals that would allow him to sit pretty during retirement. Then he and Daisy-Mae would have all the time and money in the world, and the entire globe as their playground, as they made up for lost time.

"What's got you so cheery?" Louis asked as Maverick left the ice after a particularly grueling practice.

"Nothing."

"It's a woman. Reanna contacted you?"

Maverick stopped cold. "No. Why would she?"

"What else could have you smiling like that?"

Maverick just grinned at Louis, clapped him on the back, and said, "Merry Christmas."

"Christmas isn't for another week," Louis said, falling into step behind him. "If you're thinking of cutting out early for the holidays, think again! We're on a winning streak, and I'll tan your hide if you make even one error."

"Sure thing," Maverick said with a grin that clearly baffled him.

Louis could ride him hard from now until New Year's. He didn't care. He had a date to the gala with his future fiancée tonight.

All he needed to do was keep the reporters and social influencers at bay for the next two weeks so she didn't decide an engagement wasn't necessary. He shook his head at himself and began shucking off his gear at his locker. He no longer needed to hold on to those old fears. Daisy-Mae was in it for the real thing. She wanted the ring because she loved him.

And there was no better feeling in the world.

"I TOLD Maverick to get me a ring." Daisy-Mae paced her office the next day while Violet listened.

"Wait. You're getting engaged?" Violet froze, her expression confused, her arms out like she was ready to dance if given the word.

"If things don't get crazy in the media by the new year, he is proposing. Publicly."

Violet's hands went to her mouth, her dark eyes wide. "And are you going to say yes?"

"I don't know."

"What!"

"It felt so right sitting there in the diner yesterday."

135

Violet sat. "But it doesn't feel right now?"

"I mean... Yes?" Daisy-Mae eased into the chair behind her desk.

"Don't ask me." Violet shook her head, hands held out as though she might have to ward off a clingy friend. "This is something only you and Maverick can answer. Y'all are talking about getting *married*."

Daisy-Mae sighed, a happy feeling warming her from the inside out. Married.

Wedding dresses. Invitations. Happily ever after and living in the same house with a man that made her feel happy and content.

"You love him," Violet stated.

"It's all so fast."

Violet lifted a shoulder as if to say, *So?*

"Violet! *Help* me."

"Okay. Is it real?" Violet asked. "I mean, do you have a wedding date chosen? That sort of thing? Or is this part of the fake thing?"

"He said we'd take our relationship—the real one—at my pace. But I told him to buy a ring." Daisy-Mae covered her mouth and started laughing, rocking back in her chair. When she put it like that, she couldn't even imagine what had come over her to say such a thing.

"And that felt right?" Violet confirmed.

"Yes." Daisy-Mae sighed and melted over the top of her desk, resting her head in her arms. It had felt right, but now she had to take action, had to consider the possible painful repercussions that might occur if things didn't work out or went south. She wanted to be excited, but she was scared. "He said we could have a long engagement."

"That's good. That'll help lessen the freakout factor, right?"

"But what if we break up?"

"What if you don't? *Mrs.* Blades?"

Daisy-Mae popped up from her slouch, feeling as though someone had teased her skin with a blowtorch. Mrs. Blades. Her. The Mrs.

Maverick's Mrs.

The idea made her feel faint.

"We haven't even outright said I love you, or spent the night together. And we're getting engaged?"

"Neither of you would get engaged for publicity," Violet said after a moment.

"Right?" Her friend knew her, knew how to sort through what was real and what might be just her inner freak outs.

"You both have some serious boundaries."

"We do?"

"Maverick hardly dates. You date, but never let yourself get all starry-eyed. Right now you're totally starry-eyed."

"But what if it's just a crush? Or I'm infatuated that an NHL star chose me?"

"Girl, you've known him as a star since the day he stepped on the ice. And you've been dating him for how long now? Two months? Your eyes are only getting starrier. They'd be flat by now if it'd only been a crush. You'd be complaining about him interrupting your work all the time with those *needy* texts and flowers and coffee."

"He's not needy!"

"See?" Violet crossed her arms, looking smug. "Hate to break it to you, but you two are the real deal. This big fake thing was just so you nutters could get over your hang-ups and get to the lovin' part of things."

"But Leo still needs—"

"We have our own plan. And Landon is fine. While you've been busy making goo-goo eyes at Maverick, we've all been busy, too."

"Doing what?"

Violet just smiled.

———————

MAVERICK KNEW what a beautiful woman Daisy-Mae was, but it wasn't until she was on his arm at the gala and was receiving lingering second glances from other men that he truly felt it. If they only knew how genuinely special she was, they would fight him for her.

He planted a kiss on her temple, feeling like the luckiest guy on the planet. "I love you," he whispered.

Her cheeks turned pink, and she looked up at him so full of happiness he wanted to get down on one knee and propose to her right then and there.

"I love you, too," she said, nuzzling closer.

He closed his eyes for a second, locking in the moment, the feeling of having his love returned.

"We should go home," he said. Reporters were swarming the ballroom, but tonight he wanted to escape for entirely different reasons. He wanted to have Daisy-Mae all to himself and hear her say those three sweet words over and over again.

"Why?"

"I'm greedy and selfish and want you all to myself."

She laughed, that warm smile lighting up his world.

"Maybe we should be good and go look at the auction items," she suggested.

"I don't plan on buying anything, do you?"

"No, but I feel like we're supposed to."

"Then we shall." He reminded himself that there would be many more dates and moments in their future.

They walked along the tables of items. Everything from autographed hockey sticks to exotic weekend getaways to artwork. Daisy-Mae studied everything, but he noticed she paused the longest in front of a hand-knit blanket made with about eight different colors. It would have taken a long time to create, and the current bid to beat was already over four hundred dollars.

"It's beautiful," she said, moving on. The next item was a signed jersey. His. "I have one of these." She gave him a private smile, and he understood why princes and kings gave up kingdoms for the women they loved.

"You can have as many as you like."

"Although, come to think of it, mine isn't signed."

"That can be arranged." He picked up one of the auction's pens and studied her gown. It was elegant, fitted, and looked expensive. She'd probably get mad if he tried to sign it.

She laughed, realizing what he was thinking of doing. "No way."

"Your jersey's at home? Why didn't you wear it tonight?"

"The Dragons' colors are almost black tie, but not quite. Too much gold and green in with the black, unfortunately." She took in his tuxedo, and not for the first time that he'd noticed. He had a feeling she liked what she saw.

"Maybe we should go home and sign it before we forget. I'll get the valet to bring the car around." He took her elbow, kidding but aware that he'd ditch the event if she even hinted at a yes.

She giggled. "You're such a flirt."

"Only with you." He kissed her temple again.

"Good."

"Should we go strut for the photographers?"

"You want photos tonight?" she asked, looking at him curiously. She squared her body to his, adjusting his bowtie. He was pretty sure it didn't need attention, but he liked that she was using it as an excuse to get close to him.

"May as well. We went to all of this effort to dress up."

Her smile fell and a look of concern crossed her face.

"What?" He followed her gaze over his shoulder to see Miranda, the team's owner, hurrying from the ballroom, looking upset.

He knew Daisy-Mae and Miranda were becoming friends, so he released Daisy-Mae from his loose embrace, giving her a light nudge. "Go."

She started to look up at him but was drawn back to Miranda's exit.

"Go. She's more important than my need to drag you to my lair. I'll be over there having a club soda with the guys."

She shot him a smile that hit him in the solar plexus, making him feel like he'd done the right thing by putting her friend before his caveman needs.

She doused him with a hot kiss that left him watching after her even after she'd disappeared from sight.

There was no doubt about it. Maverick Blades had lost his heart wholly and completely to Daisy-Mae Ray. And he hoped nobody planned to do a single thing about it.

———

MAVERICK CROSSED THE PORCH, the weather-worn boards creaking their hellos as a breeze tickled the hair on his arms.

"What on earth are you doing, Daisy-Mae?"

"Nothing." She gave him a guilty look and tried to stand in front of the six-foot-tall rooster she was unsuccessfully attempting to stick into the ground. It tipped over, causing her to whirl and catch it in the pre-dawn light.

"Is this my Christmas gift or is it a Christmas prank?"

"Um."

He trundled down the steps, giving her a kiss while keeping one hand on the colorful metal rooster so it didn't fall over and brain them both. He recognized the hideous beast from one of the antique shops they'd been through during their desk hunting afternoon.

"Merry Christmas," he whispered.

"Merry Christmas." She stood back as he drove the sculpture's spike into the ground, securing it in his yard. "It was supposed to be a surprise."

"I heard you drive up."

"If you hate it, plant it in someone else's yard."

"Yours?"

She laughed and squeezed his arm. She was wearing a Santa hat and her cheeks were rosy from the few minutes she'd spent out in the frosty air.

"I actually don't mind it," he said, taking a step back to assess it. "It looks better in the dark."

"Mav! It's fun."

"You're right. It is." The rooster was ridiculous, but he knew he'd never part with it.

"See? I told you it had potential. And now your dirt has some personality."

He laughed. It was true, the yard could use some serious TLC. But like the house, it would come in time.

They went inside and Maverick paused in the doorway, inhaling. His house smelled like a home. His beach house and apartment both had contained that crammed-with-newness smell. Practically everything had been met with an upgrade. The doors had barely needed a tap to close, and the appliances called for nothing more than a gentle caress to turn them on.

141

Not here. Everything had its own quirk. The dishwasher had to be bullied to keep its door closed, and even then, it often popped open mid-cycle, releasing steam and that weird dishwasher smell.

This house, with its chips and dents, scratches and worn areas held a personal history rich with memories, routines, dreams, and losses. This house was anything but impersonal. It was home, and he loved that he got to share Christmas morning in it with Daisy-Mae. Hopefully, it was the first of many.

"Come in. I made coffee." He guided her into the kitchen and poured her a cup of joe. "I got you something, too." He led her into the living room, where their tree was twinkling. The sun was rising, streaking his living room with orange and pink light.

They sat on the floor by the tree, and he pulled out the gift he'd wrapped. It had a giant bow, and the corners were pretty good considering the item inside was so soft. He probably should have put it in a box.

Watching him, Daisy-Mae pulled the corner apart, shredding the paper with a flourish. She looked down and gasped.

The multi-colored blanket she'd fallen in love with at the gala sat in her lap.

"You won this at the auction? When?" She hugged the blanket, squeezing it against her cheek. "You must have had to bid so high!"

It had taken some help from his friends to ensure that his bid was the highest at the auction's close and that Daisy-Mae didn't catch on to what he was up to.

"Thank you." She rolled up onto her knees, leaning forward to kiss him.

"There's more." He pulled out a notebook-sized box, professionally wrapped.

"Beautiful." She smoothed her hands over the paper. Her eyes were dancing as she carefully opened this one.

Inside was a chunky aquamarine necklace from her friend Jenny's shop in town, Blue Tumbleweed.

"Jenny said you've been eyeing this up."

Daisy-Mae's hands dropped, and she tipped her head to the side. "You asked my friends what I wanted?"

Of course he did.

"Want to try it on?"

She was wearing a button-up shirt and a long skirt with her Santa hat, and he scooched around so he was behind her to clasp the heavy necklace. She ran a hand over it after letting her hair back down.

"It's cold!"

"It looks good on you." He'd feared it would be too bold or big, but it looked just right on her.

It felt like something was missing, though.

He moved closer, giving her a light kiss, then brushed her shirt to the side to spy on her yellow rose tattoo above her left breast. He checked the other side in case he'd gotten confused.

"I had it removed," she said, meeting his puzzled look.

"Why?"

She shrugged.

"No, seriously. Why?" She'd had that since she was seventeen and had won a pageant after singing The Yellow Rose of Texas.

"It didn't fit my image any longer. It felt kind of trashy."

"I liked it."

"Most men did. That and the tight shirts."

"Then I hope having it removed wasn't too painful or expensive."

She gave him a kiss that grew deeper until they were making out like teenagers, sprawled on the floor by the tree, wrapped in each other's arms, the scent of pine needles filling the air.

"When was the last time you were with someone?" she asked when they came up for air, stroking his cheek with a finger.

"Intimately?" He was suddenly very aware of every soft curve of hers that was pressed against his body.

She nodded. He exhaled, thinking. It had been a long, long time. Embarrassingly long. He wasn't sure he wanted to admit the truth to Daisy-Mae.

"A year?" she asked, her tone tentative.

He didn't answer.

"Two? Three?" Her tone was becoming more incredulous. "Five?" She was laughing now, half sitting up.

He tried to act casual as he rolled onto his back, hands clasped behind his head. "Does it matter?"

Janie, about four years ago, had been his last.

Daisy-Mae straightened, obviously giving that some thought. "No," she said decisively. "I guess I was expecting that with so many women throwing themselves at you that you'd be a little busier in that department."

He watched her puzzle out his dry spell. A lot of men on the team took advantage of their popularity, but one-night stands and quickie relationships had never felt right to him.

"Why?" she asked softly, coming back to the floor to rest against him, her fist stacked on his chest as a prop for her chin.

"I don't give my trust freely. It has to be earned. And to me"—he pushed a strand of hair off her cheek—"intimacy is an act of trust. And it's difficult to build that level of trust during one date."

"Right. The One-Date Wonder," she said thoughtfully.

"I'm not great on dates, okay?" He sighed, realizing he sounded defensive.

"I'm just figuring you out."

"Sleeping with someone isn't an act I take lightly. There are consequences, and I don't ever want to find myself attached to a woman I don't like very much while we try to do something important like raise a human being together."

She nodded. Her expression was thoughtful again. "I like that. A lot."

"I'm not a prude."

"I know."

"Making love means something to me."

"There are a lot of reasons to love you, Mav. And every day I just keep on finding more."

CHAPTER 10

*D*aisy-Mae had to be crazy. And so did Maverick.

"There's nothing better than old friends," Maverick was saying into the microphone as Daisy-Mae carefully walked across the ice toward him in her cowboy boots. "And here is one of mine right now. You might know her as our mascot Dezzie's friend. Or even as someone who arranged for those free cowboy hats that five hundred of you are wearing tonight."

Cheers went up, and Daisy-Mae smiled at Maverick. What a sweetheart.

"Or as my girlfriend."

He got a few catcalls and more cheers. Fans were normally clearing out of the stands by now, racing to their cars, hoping to beat the crush of people leaving the parking lot. But many sat down again to see what was about to unfold.

Daisy-Mae was wondering the same. It was New Year's Eve. Too early for a public engagement.

Although she had suggested he surprise her. And Maverick wasn't one to disappoint. Kind of like the blanket at Christmas.

But again, a day too early.

With the microphone still held in front of him, Maverick held out his hand, waiting for her. He told the crowd he'd fallen in love, and Daisy-Mae felt an instant flash of jealousy before realizing he was talking about her.

It was then that she realized maybe he didn't think it was too soon to add his own little "something" to the team's New Year's Eve "bash" game, as arranged by the PR twins.

She almost turned back on the ice, feeling nervous. Then she caught his gaze with her own. His blue eyes were filled with fondness and love, and all of her worries and fears melted away. Before she realized it, her hand was in his. He was down on one knee there at center ice, proposing to her in front of thousands of fans.

She lost the words he was saying, her mind and heart overwhelmed. It still felt so unreal to be the recipient of his love, and she still hadn't acclimatized. And this was so big. Overwhelming, and what she'd dreamed of for so long.

He was real, and so was the giant diamond ring he was sliding onto her finger as she nodded furiously, unable to speak. The diamond had been flattened along the top, placed into white gold, and surrounded by tiny red rubies. It made her feel as if she was worthy of luxury and pampering. Her eyes dampened again. This was so much more than she deserved.

She still couldn't stop nodding.

Yes. Yes, yes, yes.

Tears wet her eyes as she slowly focused on the world around her, the cheers coming back at a deafening roar. The Dragons lined up behind Maverick, thumping their sticks on the ice. Someone with a camera edged closer, and flashes lit up the surrounding arena.

She tried to blink back the wetness so she could focus on Maverick.

She was officially off the market. Maybe for the rest of her life.

MAVERICK WAS SHAKING. Shaking like he'd just won the Stanley Cup.

He hadn't won a cup. His team wasn't at the top of their game.

But Daisy-Mae was wearing his ring.

And for some crazy reason that felt the same as winning something huge.

Maybe even one hundred percent better.

She was tearing up in a way that made his heart feel simultaneously like it might get crushed by the tightening of his ribs and lungs or simply burst out of his chest from sheer happiness.

She stepped against him again, wrapping her arms over his padded shoulders, hugging him, face buried against his jersey, shorter now because of the height of his skates. He swept her into his embrace like he had a hundred times before.

He had to remind himself this was real.

As real as the weighty diamond on her left ring finger.

She slipped her hand higher on his back and over his shoulder, peeking at the ring as they continued to hug. He had chosen something beautiful, classic, classy, sophisticated, and incredible. Her.

"I don't know if I can pull off wearing this gorgeous ring," she whispered as they pulled apart. They were on the ice, under the Jumbotron, which was likely broadcasting every nuance of their expressions.

Maverick lifted her hand, admiring the gems which fit perfectly around her slender finger.

"I think this symbolizes who you really are," he said, lifting her hand to his lips and giving her a gentle kiss. He wanted her to feel cherished, and when his eyes met hers, the tears started again. "My queen," he whispered.

She tried to hide her smile. She was happy. He quirked his head toward the crowds and she gave a shy laugh. There was no hiding how much they were crushing on each other right now. They were the stars in a show in front of thousands of people.

But it wasn't a show. It was real.

So very, very real.

They were really going to do this. All in. Full speed ahead.

Daisy-Mae, cradled in his arms, proudly held out her ring to the buzzing cameramen.

Once they'd snapped their photos, Maverick, ignoring the thousands of fans cheering them on, kissed her.

When he finally released his bride-to-be, she rocked forward in her cowboy boots, satisfyingly unseated. She had a dreamy look in her blue eyes and a drowsy half smile on her lips.

If she thought that was a kiss...just wait until they were home.

"We should get off the ice," he murmured, unable to resist planting another kiss on her lips.

She took his hand, the two of them smiling and waving, leaving the ice together. They continued down the alley to the locker rooms. As they went, he received slaps on the back, handshakes, and high fives. His teammates looked so happy for him that he felt a flicker of guilt for deceiving them about why he and Daisy-Mae had gotten together in the first place. But that was in their past now, behind them. Just a cute story about how they'd started dating. Because for him, this had always been the goal—love, then marriage.

He reached the locker room door and realized this was where his plan ended. Now he had to turn back into a teammate, ditch his fiancée, try to focus on the post-game meeting, and then shower.

That was a crappy way to propose.

"I have to help Violet out of her costume." Daisy-Mae cozied closer, her body pressed to his, as reluctant to part as he was. He resented the padding that kept him safe out on the ice for the way it currently prevented him from truly feeling her curves pressed up against him.

She rose on her tiptoes, planting a chaste, quick kiss on his lips before spinning and racing off down the corridor. Dezzie the Dragon appeared around a corner at a dead run, arms out as a loud squeal pierced the hallway and Violet tackled Daisy-Mae.

Maverick laughed. Violet's enthusiasm told him everything he needed to know about Daisy-Mae's feelings and how her friends felt about their quick proposal.

This was going to work.

———————

"WHERE WILL YOU BE GETTING MARRIED?" a reporter called out, jostling forward through the crowd. "Will it be a big wedding?"

Daisy-Mae pressed herself to Maverick's side, not because she was afraid of being trampled, but because this was their personal life and she wasn't sure how much Maverick wanted to reveal.

"It'll be…" Maverick looked to Daisy-Mae. His gaze was unfocused as though a vision for their wedding was forming in his mind, a small smile playing at his lips.

There was going to be a wedding.

Dresses. Invitations. Venue. Food.

Honeymoon.

She could picture it all. An intimate event. No press. Maybe even held in secret with only immediate family and friends since they no longer had to worry about Leo or Landon needing the positive effect from their actions.

"It'll be a private affair," he said, as though they were sharing a mental picture with each other. "As for location, maybe…" His voice trailed off.

"Somewhere special to us."

His arm tightened around her, his smile softening. "A sanctuary?" he whispered in her ear.

"Probably in Sweetheart Creek," Daisy-Mae said slowly, still watching Maverick, her voice slow. He was serious? He obviously didn't realize how intrusive a big event like that could be with tents, caterers, cleaning crews, and the works. Plus, his place wasn't even halfway renovated. How could they hold a wedding there?

Then again, she didn't really care if the house was perfect, because their love was. And that's what their wedding day would be about. The two of them.

Daisy-Mae perked up with an idea and turned to the cameras. "Actually, I have a friend, Cassandra McTavish—she's dating our goalie Landon Jackson—and she might let us hold the wedding at her lodge." She glanced at Maverick, who nodded. "Her sister also has a horse rescue ranch." She shrugged. "Maybe we'll hold it there and honor our Texas roots."

That should give them enough decoys that they could have their event in peace. And maybe drive even

Henry Wylder nuts with an onslaught of reporters around town.

More questions were hollered their way, and Maverick fielded a few. They weren't sure on a date yet— they'd only been engaged for thirty-five minutes.

Finally, someone asked the question Daisy-Mae had been dreading. "Isn't it a bit soon to get engaged? You've only been dating for a short while."

Maverick, staring Daisy-Mae straight in the eyes, said, "When you know…"

She finished his sentence. "You know."

He grinned at her.

"We've been friends most of our lives," he told the reporter. "There wasn't a lot left that I needed to learn about this amazing woman." He kissed her temple, his lips warm on her skin. "She understands me. And hockey." He grinned at the reporters who laughed and, eating it up, crowded closer again.

"Where will you live?"

"I have an addition planned for my house. There's an office where Daisy-Mae can work from on the days she doesn't commute. But that will probably become a nursery soon."

Daisy-Mae blinked. Babies were well beyond any conversation they'd had. Did he realize he'd just started what would become a frenzy of baby-bump speculation? Something like that would *not* help his image at this point. Or the team.

They were moving faster than their discussions.

Yes, she wanted to live with him. Yes, she loved he had ideas on how to fit her into his world, but wow.

"Is Daisy-Mae pregnant?" someone called out from the back of the crowd and the people in front of them jostled closer again, pressing in.

"Not yet," Maverick said. "But I'd like to start a family soon."

A family. With Maverick.

The room was starting to fade, and Daisy-Mae sagged against Maverick, struggling to stay standing, to stay focused.

Maverick pulled her against him. "Okay, that's enough for today. Thank you everyone for sharing our excitement."

Maverick guided her from the group, and she pushed away from him once they were in an empty corridor, sucking in deep breaths.

"You okay?"

"They're going to think I'm pregnant," she said, her voice tight with stress. She'd almost fainted. That would have definitely made it look as though they were planning a shotgun wedding and reinforce the idea that he was that bad boy everyone thought he was.

"Don't you think you should have discussed some of that stuff with me?" She bent over, letting the dizziness wane.

"Sorry, I got swept up in the dream." He was watching her, smiling, completely oblivious.

"They're going to swarm me. They're going to talk about my weight, and if I wear anything baggy, they'll say you're marrying me for the baby. And then if I'm skinny the next day, they'll say I lost the baby due to stress of being engaged to The One-Date Wonder."

His smile turned to concern.

They were silent for a long moment, and she felt the tension rising between them. She didn't want to fight. She didn't want the world stepping in and messing up one of the most beautiful moments she'd ever had.

She straightened, looking at him. "It's a beautiful dream." Her eyes filled with tears. It was a dream she'd never allowed herself to believe in because of how deeply it would crush her when it failed to happen.

Maverick opened his arms, and she fell into them with a sob.

"Why are you crying?" he asked, stroking her hair.

"I'm overwhelmed!" She pushed back so she could look at him, but he wouldn't release her. He looked confused.

"You said to buy you a ring. And to surprise you."

"After New Year's!"

"That wouldn't have been a surprise. And what's waiting another two hours, so it's after midnight?"

She laughed. His thinking was so linear sometimes. She rested her head against his chest. "Mav?"

"Hm?"

"Are we really getting married? Or is this just part of the deal?"

"I'd never fake something that important."

CHAPTER 11

"Where are you?" Maverick held his phone to his ear, taking in Daisy-Mae's office on Monday morning. He could barely see her desk's surface, so many bouquets of flowers were crowding it. The wall to his right was partially hidden by a stack of delivery boxes and wrapped gifts.

There'd been nothing at his house. The only traffic down his gravel road was himself, his hired hand, and the occasional brave courier driver who delivered something that far out of town when he saw Maverick's name on the package. He'd stopped doing that, though, and instead ordered everything under a pseudonym or to his mother's.

Which meant Daisy-Mae was likely getting all of their gifts. Then again, he hadn't been in the locker room yet today. He made a note to get there before the rest of the team so they wouldn't tease him too hard if it was even a quarter as overwhelming as Daisy-Mae's office.

"I'm working from home."

"Why?" He nudged aside some lilies and set down the coffees he'd bought for them to share.

"I couldn't get in."

"Something wrong with your car?"

"No, it's insane there. I got swarmed."

Maverick moved to the window of her fourth-floor office, peering down at the crowd of reporters blocking the front doors.

"Didn't you use your pass to go in the private entrance?" The building had a fenced and gated private lot in the back, which was monitored by a security guard.

"That's for players and management."

"That's you." Before she could protest, he added, "You have an ID card, don't you?" Not like security wouldn't know who she was. Men noticed Daisy-Mae, and any employee worth their salt would definitely know her now, thanks to her very public engagement to the team's captain.

"I didn't realize I could park back there."

Maverick smiled. Even if you tried, you couldn't take the down-home gal out of a woman like Daisy-Mae. It was one of the reasons he adored his fiancée so much.

Fiancée. He was still getting used to calling her that. It had only been four days, but the word hadn't lost its powerful kick.

"Are you in my office?" she asked.

"I am. The place looks like a florist's. You have a lot of gifts, too."

"*We* do."

He moved over to the wall and began reading the tags, telling her who some of the gifts were from. Maverick chuckled with fondness at a familiar name.

"Who's that?"

"The first referee to eject me from a game. He says on here that you'll need this." He nudged the box, curious what was inside.

"Do you want to bring some gifts home with you?"

He eyed the room. "I didn't drive my truck today."

"It's that crazy?"

"Understatement." It was flattering but not surprising. The world loved Daisy-Mae almost as much as he did.

He put her on speaker while he sorted a few gifts into a come-home-tonight pile. "How's your new desk working out?"

"Don't laugh, but I'm actually working on the couch." Before he could say he'd told her so, she said quickly, "But it's only because I keep getting deliveries here, too. The couch is closer to the door."

"And awesome to work from," he pointed out.

"The desk is okay, but it feels...I don't know. Formal."

"Are you going to work from home more often?"

"The commute has lost its thrill. Especially since I'm no longer sharing it with Violet."

"I hear you." And it would be even less thrilling once they started a family. But he couldn't see either of them living in the city permanently. He'd only been back in the country for a few months but had no plans to leave. "So, what are you gonna do?"

"Miranda said I can try working from home until it settles down a bit. So here I am, I guess. Then I was thinking if I can swing it financially, Vi and I can get a little holiday trailer for in the city. Although she doesn't sound as keen as she did a few weeks ago."

With Violet? What about him?

"A holiday trailer?" He envisioned it parked behind the arena, sort of like trailers for actors when they were working on location.

"Just something simple and cute. Not one of those big monstrosities. You can get an old one for pretty cheap, and then you park them in a campground and pay a monthly rate—"

"No." He almost laughed, but over the years he'd figured out Daisy-Mae worked a lot of jobs, not for a lack of things to do. She wasn't raking in millions of dollars a year like he was. "You're the fiancée of an NHL star. You're almost a celebrity." He wondered if that warm gooey feeling in his chest whenever he thought of her as his fiancée would ever fade. He hoped not. He peeked through the blinds again. "We'll get an apartment close by." Another car pulled up, and a cameraman got out. "With a doorman."

She laughed. "I can't suddenly afford a nice place just because I'm engaged to you."

"We need to protect your privacy. These reporters are here for you."

"Because you made them think I'm pregnant!"

"Sorry about that." He cringed, knowing his mouth had gotten way ahead of any plans they had.

This morning he'd read the speculation online about how far along she might be. The two of them were getting press like he'd predicted. Just not quite the kind they'd wanted. Although overall, everyone seemed excited by the idea that she might be expecting. One article had even run a poll on some possible baby names. Personally, he was rooting for Brayton if it was a boy.

"Leo was saying there's an opening in his building. I'll check it out."

"This job is my only income stream, Mav. If I screw up—"

"What are you talking about? You won't screw up."

"But if I do…"

"Won't happen."

"What if all my ideas dry up? I mean, once we have this fan stuff all working, it's just rinse and repeat…" Sadness filled her voice. "What will they need me for? I haven't even been to college. I'd be the first to get the ax when they're looking to trim my department."

Maverick paused, considering his words before deciding to simply be blunt. "Are you freaking out?"

"No!"

"Come on, Froggy."

She sighed at the nickname.

"Tell me."

"I'm just overwhelmed."

"Yeah?" He sat in one of her chairs and crossed an ankle over his knee, pulling one of the coffees from the lilies and taking a sip. "Pour it all on me."

"Everything's so fast, and everyone wants to know our plans. I'm used to having everything laid out and various speeches at the ready when there's this kind of attention. In pageants I was prepared for the onslaught and it was predictable and short-lived." Her voice shook. "I don't know where we're getting married or when I'm moving in or even where we'll live. How many kids we want? I don't even know how to act like your fiancée."

"Just be yourself."

Her voice was small when she said, "I don't know how to do this. It's not just walk on stage and smile at the lights, then go back home to being a nobody. This is...constant."

Maverick's heart dropped, and he sat forward. He checked his watch, calculating how quickly he could make it to her side. He had an afternoon practice, and the soonest he could be there to help settle and reassure her wouldn't be until after supper.

They needed to get married sooner rather than later.

He also needed to fix this. And the first thing he could do was buy her some privacy and downtime.

"I'll get us an apartment in the city and hire a driver

for the days we don't want to drive back home," he said. "I'll bring some of these gifts back to Sweetheart Creek tonight. Then we'll sit down and figure out the details and make a plan. We'll have a united front to present to those who ask.

"The publicity is good. It's friendly. Just put on your beauty queen persona and smile and wave. We'll get through this. They love you. And they love us together."

She sighed. "Mav, they're going to figure out that I'm poor and uneducated. I'm so afraid I'm going to screw up without even realizing it. This is a different world for me."

"Whoa. You're doing amazing things here at work and nobody is saying otherwise. You're amazing." Sensing she wasn't fully convinced, he added, "You're the only one to break my one-date rule in over four years, you know. That says a lot."

"Yeah, because Louis said he'd kick you off the team if you didn't stick with me."

He laughed with her, moving back to the window. The crowd showed no hints of subsiding. "Okay, so maybe there was some outside pressure to kick us into gear. But we didn't have any problems agreeing to a second date. Remember?"

"I guess I broke your rule, didn't I?" There was a smile in her voice, and Maverick felt like he could breathe again.

He lowered his voice. "But also, I want you to know that *never*, not even for one hot second, did I *ever* want to back out of a date with you."

There was authority and confidence in her voice again when she said, "We can't move in together. Not until we're married."

"You're worried about our reputations?"

"It already looks like a shotgun wedding or entrapment."

He sat down hard, finally understanding. Daisy-Mae wasn't afraid of the attention. She was afraid that people might see her in the way her mother did—that she was desperate and poor, and looking for a flashy life and had trapped him with a pregnancy. She saw herself as some small-town gal punching above her heart's pay grade when in his mind he was too.

"Fine. Separate places until we get married. But you need a place closer to work, and because this is my mess, I'm paying for it all."

She didn't argue, and he considered it a win.

"Just, you know, don't stretch out the engagement, okay?"

"Don't worry," she said warmly, "I'll be the good wife. I'll wait until you're legally obligated to me before I bankrupt you."

He laughed, knowing she'd never do such a thing, but his heart warmed as her voice turned more upbeat again.

There was just one more thing to put the icing on the cake.

"Hey, Daise?"

"Hm?"

"Landon got an offer this morning. A really sweet one."

_____

"No." Maverick turned to Louis, who wouldn't meet his eye. He turned back to Reanna. "This is my interview."

He was missing his morning coffee in Daisy-Mae's office for this. And with things extra busy since their engagement two weeks ago, he didn't want to miss a single moment with her. His agent had been fielding calls, and there were a lot of pulls on his time right now. It was a good thing Daisy-Mae understood his lifestyle, the fame, the busyness. She'd helped him get here, after all.

The season was ending in just a few months, and there would be one more thing off his plate until training. They'd have more time, and everything would work out beautifully again.

Except for this.

"Actually, it's my interview," Reanna stated calmly.

Maverick turned to Louis again, who gave a sheepish shrug. "You ambushed me? You lied? I'm the sideshow in *her* interview? I was supposed to be talking about the season ahead and our winning streak. What is this?"

Louis pulled him aside. "She's agreeing to talk about things publicly. She's going to clear your name of any wrongdoing."

"Too little, too late." He paced one way, then the other. He faced Louis again. "So now that I'm finally getting my life and career repaired and people are forgetting, she wants to stir it up? She's going to tell the world we didn't have an affair. Who's going to believe that?"

"It's worth a try, isn't it?"

"For what?" Maverick asked. "I'm fine. Finally. I have an offer for a commercial. I have my health. I could retire tonight and be okay. I don't see any reason to go on screen with her."

"Can you please do it for the rest of the guys on the team?"

"They don't need me. Getting engaged to Daisy-Mae increased my likability, and I'm *happy*. Isn't that enough?"

"I need this." Louis locked his gaze on Maverick's, staring at him in a way that had him second-guessing his stance. He glanced toward Reanna, who was being fitted for a lapel microphone, getting comfortable on the white couch set in front of the cityscape backdrop. This was supposed to be his interview.

"Daisy-Mae isn't here," Maverick stated, crossing his arms.

"This doesn't concern her."

"I think it does."

"If she were here," Louis said, carefully steering Maverick toward the soundstage, "it would look as if Reanna was apologizing to your fiancée for going around with you behind her back."

Louis had a point.

"This is clean. PR has vetted all the questions."

"I don't like this."

"Miranda thinks it's a good idea. A push to get you even higher. The *team* higher. Your team, Captain."

"Seriously. Could you guilt me a little more?" All Louis needed to do next was bring up his mom and the crap she'd had to deal with.

His coach was giving him that steely look again. It was one he used on unruly rookies just before he benched them for half a season or bag skated them for weeks on end so they learned he was the boss.

Wait a second. "Why are *you* here?" Louis was in his coaching gear, not likely to be on screen.

"One minute!" called someone from over by the large cameras.

Maverick and Louis stared at each other for a long moment.

"When have I ever steered you wrong?"

Maverick sighed, unable to think of a single time. Even dating Daisy-Mae—as crazy as the setup had seemed—had been a smart move. In all ways.

"Fine. But put it on record that I hate this idea and I'm against it." He pointed at Louis. "If things go to crap, it's all on you."

"That's my boy," Louis said, stepping back as stage-hands pulled Maverick onto the set, clipping him with a microphone and directing him to sit on the couch. They tried to place him close to Reanna, but he made sure there was as much room as humanly possible. When the cameraman asked him to move further to the left, closer to Reanna, he glowered and told him to shoot from a different angle.

Reanna shifted uncomfortably, and her throat moved as she swallowed hard. Without looking at him, she said quietly, "I'm doing this so Daisy-Mae knows what a good man you are."

"She knows without you having to tell her that. She said yes to my marriage proposal, after all."

Maverick considered leaving.

"We're on air in ten seconds," someone commanded from beyond the bright lights shining on them. The show's host appeared, quickly shaking hands and getting settled.

The intro went fast, and then the host was turning to Reanna with the first question. "You're here today to clear the air about something, is that right?"

"Yes," Reanna said, her voice wavering and low.

Maverick closed his eyes, hoping the camera wasn't on him. Was she going to blow it? She hadn't had the courage to step away from her husband and seek help a year ago. Had things changed enough that she wouldn't bail at the last minute?

"You're here because you've left your husband, Adwin Kendrik, the owner of the NHL team The La-fayette Blur?"

"Yes."

"You're also here because you're coming forward about something you've kept private for many years. Would you like to tell us about it?"

Reanna inhaled sharply, and there was a painful

moment of silence before she began talking. "My husband was abusive. He would get angry and hurt me. I'm not here to call him out on that. I'm here to clear a good friend's name and reputation."

Maverick nearly snorted. Good friend? He hadn't heard from her in months, and she'd ambushed him to get him here instead of speaking to him like a reasonable human being. She'd ruined him and left him hanging.

He understood her actions, but to call him a good friend was an outright lie.

"I behaved in a way that hurt Maverick Blades." She reached for his hand across the space, but he stared straight ahead, keeping his hands clasped between his knees. "He was there for me. The times that the press photographed us together were times he was protecting me. Taking me to a safe place—a-a-a hotel."

Well, that sounded bad. Apparently, her answers to the questions hadn't been vetted.

"He stepped in when I wasn't safe. He knew what was going on with me and Adwin, and he helped me stay safe."

"Maverick?" The host turned to him. "Did you ever go to the authorities on Reanna's behalf?"

"She begged me not to. She felt the risk to her safety was too great."

"Could you elaborate why?" The host turned back to Reanna. "Maybe help other women who are listening and find themselves in the same situation?"

"I-I-I'd lose everything if I left Adwin."

"How so?"

"Everything was in his name. I had nothing. And he told me that's what I'd get if I ever left him or went to the police. He threatened to hide our assets so I'd never get a dime."

"But your safety..." the host asked.

"Maverick tried to help me leave, but the press skewered him." She stared straight at the reporter. "Adwin targeted him and his career."

Maverick sent up a silent prayer that she wouldn't cause him any new enemies, both in the world of the NHL and with the press.

"I was so caught up in my own world I didn't fully understand what was happening to Maverick. He took the brunt, but I couldn't step up and say that things were..." She closed her eyes for a moment. "The rumors made it bad at home, and I was afraid if I said anything—anything at all—about what was going on with Maverick and Adwin that everything would come out and that I'd get hurt. Badly."

"And what about Maverick?" the reporter asked gently. "He was hurt."

A tear escaped Reanna's left eye.

The reporter turned to Maverick. "You almost lost your career?"

Maverick gave a small nod. He didn't want to talk about it, but seeing as Reanna was having a breakdown to his left, he continued. "My reputation took a hit, and people have treated me differently. I was traded, and I was pretty close to losing my career this year. Thankfully, the Dragons are doing a lot better than we were at the beginning of our season." He smiled, trying to lighten the mood. Reanna was sobbing quietly, and he wasn't sure what to do. Nobody had prepped him for this. He didn't want to add to Reanna's burden, but he wanted this stupid reporter to know that he and his colleagues had damaged his career.

"I think the worst part is that a lot of people assume the worst of me. People who didn't know me." And some who did.

"Do you regret keeping your silence?"

"I think stepping forward would've made things

worse. Not just for Reanna, but for myself. Nobody would've believed me, especially when I couldn't say why I was taking a married woman into a hotel. Even though I always left a few minutes later. There were never timestamps on any of the images that were published." He stared at the host for a minute. "I'm sure there are people who will watch this today and won't believe us. That's the power of the press. People believe you when it's more interesting than the truth."

The host toyed with his question cards, skipping one.

"I told Reanna I'd keep her secret, keep her safe, and give her time so she could extract herself. Going public was never my call to make." He turned to Reanna. "And I'm glad that you're in a safe place now."

"He's suing me," she said, her voice tight. "I'll get nothing. I should have left earlier."

Maverick turned back to the host, afraid he'd say something he'd regret.

"You seem very calm," the host said. "Are you angry?"

He saw a flash of Louis's jacket out of the corner of his eye and caught himself before falling into the trap that was being laid. *NHL Star Angry at the Decimation of his Reputation!*

"If I could go back in time, would I have chosen a different path? No. I have a mother. I have a fiancée. Both are women I love very much. If someone was hurting them and there was somebody who could step in and help but didn't because it might come at a personal sacrifice...?" He shook his head. "Sure, I sometimes wish someone else had stumbled upon Reanna and her problems." He gave a weak smile before growing serious again. "But I'm not the kind of man to turn his back. And I'm lucky I have a woman who knows who I am and loves me. She didn't need this show to tell her why."

They went to break, and Maverick removed his microphone. Without saying goodbye to Reanna, he stood and walked out, his quads shaking with pent-up anger. There was only one person he wanted to spend his time with right now, and if he was lucky, maybe he could still catch her for a late morning coffee.

"SORRY, I have to take this. It's my agent again."

Daisy-Mae nodded, understanding that this was part of the package of Maverick's amended reputation and their public engagement.

Maverick stepped outside the Longhorn Diner to take the call.

Over half a dozen offers for various deals had come in since Reanna's little tell-all to the press last week. They'd paid her sweetly for her story, of course.

Various outlets had approached Maverick to tell his side of the story, but he'd declined. Thankfully. Things had turned into a full-on zoo since Reanna went public.

And thanks to Daisy-Mae mentioning the Peppermint Lodge after her engagement, Cassandra was also being swarmed. Although, they were all offering to help at the Ray-Blades wedding.

They didn't even have a date yet and, at this rate, were more likely to elope like Miranda had on New Year's Eve. And that would be lame. She failed to understand the appeal of modern elopements.

Frankly, though, the attention on her and Maverick was overwhelming. The worst of it was feeling like a third wheel around him. She hadn't thought about what it might be like once they'd mended his reputation and the world saw him the way she did. Sometimes she wondered if he even needed her any longer. Which was silly thinking because he loved her and was marrying her—eventually. He was just really, really busy.

Daisy-Mae continued eating her salad and garlic bread, waving over Mrs. Fisher.

"Can I get a refill, please?" She tapped her empty glass of sweet tea.

"You betcha, hon. How are things going?" She tipped her head toward the window where they could see Maverick pacing on the sidewalk out front, ear to his phone.

"Good. How are you?"

"That man hasn't been able to sit down and finish a meal all week."

They'd only been in three times, Maverick determined to shoehorn in coffee or a semi-proper date with her. She appreciated his efforts, but Mrs. Fisher was right. His phone never stopped ringing, whether they were in for a quick coffee or a meal. Daisy-Mae had suggested Maverick's agent stack up the list of things he wanted to talk about and do it all in one call. But apparently he already was.

And since Maverick was looking at some sizeable deals, Daisy-Mae didn't want to get in the way of him striking while the iron was hot. Some of them could set him up for the rest of his life.

By the time Daisy-Mae finished her meal, Maverick returned. He sat across from her, looked at her empty plate, then down at his own untouched meal. "I'm sorry."

"It's fine."

His phone rang again, but he silenced it.

"You need to answer that."

"No, I need to pay attention to you."

"Your attention is going to be on what you might've

missed by not taking that call. Go ahead. Take it out-side. I'll have Mrs. Fisher pack up your meal."

Maverick's smile tightened. He didn't seem happy, but he complied.

Daisy-Mae waved down Mrs. Fisher to pay for supper and get Maverick's boxed. While she waited, she tried to remember what her father had told her at the away game earlier in the week. He'd been passing through on a trucking route, and Maverick had scored them both front row seats to watch him play. Her father had loved being so close to the action, and he'd let it slip that he admired her patience. When she'd ex-pressed her confusion, he'd explained that it was easy to jump into something with someone. It was a lot harder to wait, to trust, to believe that the right person was going to come along and that you'd find that en-during soul-level love.

He believed she'd been waiting, not that nobody wanted her. How could her two parents see her so dif-ferently? His words, along with Maverick's efforts to spend time with her, had lifted her up, made her re-member that all of this insanity was worth it. She'd waited. And she'd been rewarded with the right man.

This insanity was just...temporary. Difficult, but temporary.

"Hey, stranger." Laura, Levi Wylder's fiancée, slid into the seat across from Daisy-Mae as Mrs. Fisher set down Maverick's packaged meal. Laura was a retired fashion model who was brokering deals around the globe as she wet her entrepreneurial feet. She reached across the table, her eyes lighting up at Daisy-Mae's ring. "I haven't even said congratulations yet! You've been so busy."

"I know. You too. Hey, how was..." Daisy-Mae tried to recall the last place she'd heard Laura had gone but realized she was well out of the loop.

Laura waved off the question. Her gaze flicked to Maverick through the window, then back to Daisy-Mae. "I couldn't help but notice that Maverick's coming up in the world—lots of deals and attention right now?"

Daisy-Mae nodded, careful not to show her current annoyance with how busy it kept him. She was lucky. She was grateful.

"It's tough."

"What is?"

"It's just tough." Laura pulled her hands into the sleeves of her sweater. "You've got this new relationship and then suddenly your life explodes in the way you had been hoping it would for years. But the timing is sucky."

"Oh, I'm sorry." Her belief that Laura had been empathizing quickly turned to concern. "I thought you and Levi were splitting time between being on the road and at the ranch?"

Last she'd heard, his brothers Myles and Cole had stepped in to fill the hole their older brother was leaving each time he went away with Laura. It had sounded as though it was working well for everyone.

"We are. And it's great." Her face had lit up at the mention of Levi's name. Daisy-Mae wondered if she did that when someone mentioned Maverick.

"Oh. Then good."

"But it's not always easy. And it was a definite adjustment for both of us. Especially Levi. He was such a hermit." She laughed, her affection obvious. "You should have seen him in New York the first time. He looked so uncomfortable."

She reached over and gave Daisy-Mae's hand a tight squeeze. "Hang in there. It'll all settle out. Love is worth the bumps in the road." She leaned back again, her tone slightly scolding. "But make sure you speak up for what you want. Boundaries are important. It's too early for you to…" She stopped, smiled, then shook her head as though tossing away the advice she'd been about to give.

Daisy-Mae let out a shaky breath. "Too early for me to feel resentment?"

Laura gave Daisy-Mae's hand another squeeze. "Just be patient and keep the lines of communication open. Be kind. Be honest." She returned to her spot across the room where she'd been having supper with April Wylder.

Daisy-Mae took a moment to collect herself, then gathered her purse and Maverick's meal. Things would settle out. They'd find a new pattern and it would all be okay.

At the door, she met Maverick as he was coming back in.

She took one look at him and braced herself for more disappointment. "What's wrong?"

He inhaled, looking down the street before shutting his eyes tight, then releasing them to look back at her. "I have to go."

"What do you mean?" They were supposed to be having supper, then going through the wedding invitation samples and then head to Cassandra's to consider her lodge as their venue. This was the second time they'd had to cancel.

"That campaign for the skates. Their photographer has emergency surgery booked in two days and wants to squeeze me in now, so the whole thing doesn't get pushed back by a month."

Daisy-Mae tried to remember what his schedule was like and what this change might mean.

"I have to fly to New York tonight. Tomorrow morning we're doing the shoot."

"But you practice tomorrow morning."

It wasn't like him to miss practice. Not for money.

"I can miss one."

Was it just one, though? She feared it was the thin edge of the wedge.

"Why can't they hire a different photographer?"

They had planned their wedding around hockey. Their *wedding*. And now this was pushing aside their wedding planning *and* hockey?

"I don't like this." She caught herself. "But it's not my decision, not my career. So, go. Get the photos taken."

"I'm sorry."

"Are you going to call Cassandra and tell her we're canceling again?" If he was the one always pulling out, he needed to be the one facing the disappointment from everyone. Yes, as his partner, she should be more giving, but she was working two jobs and commuting several days a week as well. Plus trying to plan their late-spring wedding with him.

It was like Laura said, boundaries.

If she kept taking over more and more things from his life, she'd soon be drowning. If he was saying yes to every deal that came across his agent's desk and expecting her to bend around it all, then he at least had to sort out how to make it all happen. She wasn't his assistant, and that wasn't the kind of relationship she wanted to have with the man.

"Anything you decide with Cassandra is fine by me." He planted a kiss on the top of her head.

"No. No way. I am not planning our wedding without you. If you don't help, there is no wedding."

"Daisy-Mae," he said with a hint of impatience.

"No. Because right now, I don't even know if you would be able to carve out the date and make it."

Maverick looked at her in shock.

"I am not your mother or your assistant. I can't be superwoman. I'm not willing."

173

He looked miffed.

"I like to think I'm supportive. I come to your away games when I can. I flex my schedule around your practices and games so we can sit and chat or commute together. But I can't do all of this. I'm not going to put my entire life on hold--"

"I'm not asking you to."

She felt the statement hit her like it was the lead-in to a breakup speech.

"Look, we're a team," he said, the vein on his forehead bulging. "I got you that apartment because you needed it, and it would make your life easier. I'm not even staying there because you don't like how it might look to the public. And I appreciate you looking out for me. I really do. But I need you to help me out a little, too."

Daisy-Mae closed her eyes, realizing he had a point.

He didn't want to break up, he was just frustrated too. They both needed to give and take, and he was doing his best even if it felt like it wasn't enough.

It was all just so exhausting.

"I'll talk to Cassandra. But the next appointment we make with her needs to be in pen. Not pencil. And maybe..." She waited until she had his full attention, hating that she was about to suggest this. "Maybe we need to push the wedding date back. Just until things settle down."

CHAPTER 12

Daisy-Mae shifted uncomfortably, checking her phone for a miracle I'll-be-there-after-all text from Maverick. Even though she knew he was still in the city, even though the wedding ceremony would be starting at any moment.

He was supposed to be here, though. She'd chosen his tie to match her aquamarine dress. All based on his gorgeous eyes. She'd been looking forward to today. Just the two of them—finally—celebrating Valentine's Day at a wedding. But a last-minute meeting change followed by an additional commitment, and he wouldn't make it back to town until the reception.

She understood. She really did.

But that didn't mean she didn't feel the sting. It was too easy to feel like she wasn't important enough to have him say no—just once—to a work commitment so he could keep one with her.

She'd seen the conflict in his eyes when he'd told her he'd be late. The hesitation. She hadn't been sure if he was asking permission or worried she'd have a meltdown. He sure hadn't liked her suggestion to move their wedding date back a few months, and the idea had introduced a new tension to their relationship. She'd tried to explain that she wanted their wedding to be special, not rushed or jammed between commitments and games. She wanted them to be present, relaxed, and to truly enjoy their day.

She was pretty sure he'd understood. Mostly. He seemed impatient to get another ring on her finger and had even suggested elopement.

Hard no on that one. Her friends April and Brant had eloped and then ended up having a big party later —basically a wedding. So what was the point of eloping?

Her phone showed no new messages, not even a "thinking of you" text. That meant Maverick was already filming his interview with the sports station, or that he'd fallen asleep somewhere after finishing filming the predawn commercial. At least he had a car service bringing him out to Sweetheart Creek, so she didn't have to worry about him falling asleep behind the wheel.

She'd helped him get to this level, but she hadn't realized what it would feel like once they were here. Insanely busy, everyone wanting his time, the pressure to make hay while the sun still shone on his corner of the ice.

"Did he forget?" her mother asked from her spot in the pew beside her.

"No."

"It's Valentine's Day. Your first one together."

"I know," she said tightly, her nails digging into her palms.

They were silent for a long moment, gentle music filling the church as more guests found their seats.

"Did you two break up?" her mom asked abruptly. She was looking straight ahead, acting as though she hadn't uttered a thing. People snuck peeks over their shoulders, curious what the reaction—and answer—was to her mother's question.

"No, we did not," Daisy-Mae said loud enough for the eavesdroppers.

"Is he back with that Reanna woman? I saw them in an interview. They seemed pretty close to me."

"Please stop."

"Once a cheater, always a cheater."

"He's not a cheater!" she said, her patience snapping, her voice too loud. People turned to look even as the groomsmen took their places at the front of the church. A lineup of dark-haired men with blue eyes, all in their new cowboy boots—the Wylder brothers—watched her with concern.

At one point, she'd thought the men would become her brothers, her family. And right now they no doubt feared she was causing a scene.

Daisy-Mae looked away, embarrassed. She bit her tongue to help her focus on something other than the swell of unexplained emotion building inside her. It was bad enough that Maverick, after inviting her to be his date, had canceled on her. Now she was here like an old maid on Valentine's Day, sitting beside her mom who was back to her tired games of wishing her love life ill-will.

Daisy-Mae slid down the pew, putting space between herself and her mother. *Control the things you can, right?*

She kept her eyes up front, ignoring the looks her mother was surely shooting her way.

The music changed and a flower girl walked down the aisle, tossing rose petals over her own head and squealing with delight. Then the bridesmaids: Jackie, April, Laura, and Carly. Karen's soon-to-be sisters-in-law. They looked beautiful in their pale blue dresses.

Her mother spun, eyeing Daisy-Mae from head to

foot, then again, eyes narrowed. Daisy-Mae looked down at her dress and panic set in.

Oh, no. Oh, no no no no.

Her dress was almost the same shade of blue as the gals. It looked like she was trying to shoehorn her way into something like the wedding party.

She had to leave. Now.

She started scrambling for the aisle closest to the wall, but a couple had squeezed in while she'd been watching the bridesmaids. They smiled warmly, the woman's gaze straying to Daisy-Mae's flat midriff, then back up to her eyes as though she might see the truth in them. Daisy-Mae sighed and looked away. It was either squeeze past them or her mother and possibly draw notice and start some gossip, or sit here and lump it.

She really wished Maverick was here.

How had she not known their colors?

Because she'd been too busy with her job and big fiancé to know what her friends were going to be wearing today.

Taking a deep breath, she straightened. She'd go home as soon as the ceremony was over, change her dress. Come back when Maverick arrived. Nobody would notice. She'd zip out super fast, not talk to a soul.

Karen came down the aisle, her eyes only on Myles. He was beaming in a way she'd never seen before. They were like two magnets drawn together. Meant to be.

No running around like madmen, barely snatching moments together.

Had she been reckless in refusing to plan the wedding without Maverick? It was already February, and they'd put off more meetings and appointments than they'd kept. She sighed. Things with Maverick, when she was feeling extra tired and neglected, reminded her of a dreaded, familiar holding pattern. She knew Maverick loved her, truly loved her, but it was still easy to feel as though she and their relationship weren't a priority. Especially since he didn't need her to fix his image any longer and was out there rebuilding his life on his own. So much time alone.

Myles and Karen kissed, the music starting up again. As soon as the married couple was through the church doors, Daisy-Mae was on her feet, pressing against the wall, eager to escape so she could save face.

––––––––

"YOU'RE NEVER AROUND."

"I know. I'm sorry. But it's not forever."

Daisy-Mae looked upset. She'd been acting like this from the moment she appeared at the reception in her red dress. Why had she bought him this greenish-blue tie to match her if she was wearing red?

He'd had to phone her when he arrived because nobody had seen her. What on earth was going on with his gregarious girlfriend?

"What do you want me to do, Daisy-Mae?" Maverick lowered his voice. "Say no to the deals?"

She didn't reply as she took a long swallow of champagne.

Daisy-Mae had wanted his success and had helped him even when he hadn't wanted it for himself. She was someone who didn't mind bending her schedule and making the effort. She found a way to be there with him. But now she was acting like she resented it. It was eerie how much it reminded him of Janie.

He understood Daisy-Mae's point of view, though. Things had suddenly exploded on them, and the past several weeks had been overwhelming and tiring, a drain on them both. But they were a team. A darn good one.

179

Still, her mood today felt a bit left field, and it concerned him that maybe he'd misread their situation. Maybe he'd been correct when he assumed he couldn't do the all-out, big-time hockey life *and* keep a woman happy. They both needed so much time and devotion.

"I thought you wanted me to say yes to these deals."

"Maverick..." She looked at him as though he was being a ridiculous, obtuse man. And maybe he was, but this was his Daisy-Mae. She understood. So why was she unhappy? She knew this busy phase wouldn't last forever and that he loved her.

Realizing they were drawing attention, he took her hand. "Let's step outside." She clutched her champagne to her chest as he led her away from the groups of people milling about in the old Sweetheart Creek community barn, out the doors and around to the side where guests wouldn't be parking in the grass or smoking and interrupting them.

"Seriously, Daise," he said. "What would you like me to do? I only have a bit more of this and few more years of hockey."

"I can't *take* a few more years."

"Of...me?"

"Hockey stuff! The extras. You're never around."

"This is setting us up for the rest of our lives."

Her lower lip trembled. "I can't take any more."

"Specifically—what is it that you can't take any more of?" He crossed his arms despite his efforts to stay calm, stay open, stay patient. Tonight was the one night he had to hang out all week. And next week, too. He'd been looking forward to dancing with her, laughing, holding her hand. Just her and their friends. All night. Making memories. Picking up ideas for their own wedding. Letting their hair down and just...being.

"*This* is like Myles all over again. Everything else

comes first. I feel like I'm being held on to until you know that you no longer need me."

He let out a harsh sound of disbelief. "Myles? You think I'm like Myles? The guy who, after a decade, still wouldn't commit to you?" He felt the rage building. "I'm *nothing* like him. Do you know he didn't even know if you were the one? How does a man not know that?" He jabbed a thumb toward his chest. "I have *always* known."

Her lashes were wet, creating little star shapes around her baby blues. He stepped back, forcing himself to remain calm, aware he was likely making things worse.

"Then why don't you ever make me a priority? Now that your old life is back, you never have time for me or our commitments. You weren't even here for the ceremony. And I'm your date!"

"You said it was okay."

"What was I supposed to say? No? Be unsupportive of what you're trying to do with your career just because I want my fiancé at my side on our first Valentine's Day? That I'm too scared to show up at my ex's wedding alone?"

"Yes! You're supposed to be honest with me."

"I'm so out of the loop that I showed up in a dress the same color as the bridesmaids—my friends. Women who were supposed to be my sisters."

Supposed to be her sisters.

It was about Myles. She was losing Myles today.

He'd thought she was over him, that their love was enough.

Maverick inhaled slowly, willing his voice to come out calm and neutral. "Do you still love him?"

She looked so insulted he apologized. "Okay. Then what?"

"This..." She waved at the barn. Music had started

181

up. Good old two-stepping music. "*Family*. I dreamed about this day and it's just…"

Her expression was so forlorn, and he didn't know how to fix it. He wasn't from a big family like she craved. He had no siblings. He didn't even know where his dad lived anymore.

"It feels like our wedding isn't…" She let out a jagged sigh, then sniffed.

He'd assumed she felt the certainty and depth of their love like he did. He'd believed she'd be okay here alone today, among family and friends as part of her community. She was the woman who took on protesters. She didn't crumble. What was this all truly about?

"It's Valentine's Day, Mav."

He sighed and pulled her into his arms, sighing in relief. Valentine's Day. He'd almost forgotten about the date, and she must have sensed it. He kissed the top of her head. "I got you flowers. Didn't they get delivered?"

"No, but it's not about flowers," she grumbled. She didn't soften into his arms like usual, and he stepped back, looking at her. He sensed that they needed to set their sights straight again. They were a team. They had a common goal to focus on.

"This is my life right now, and it's not forever. I don't want to sound harsh, but this is what you signed on for. You signed up to help me get to this place. And now I'm here. We're in the show we set our sights on."

He wanted to ask her if she was still with him, if she was in. But he was afraid of what her answer might be.

"I guess I forgot that this was all just some show." She turned and strode away, her dress snapping at her calves.

Maverick watched her go, confused, as his image of what tonight was supposed to be like faded with the setting sun.

"What's wrong?" Myles asked. He was in his tuxedo, bowtie still in place, which was unlike him. He gestured with his chin, pointing toward the barn where music was blasting as the reception gained its party momentum.

"Nothing." Daisy-Mae straightened, willing her damp eyes to act like the Sahara and dry up.

Honestly, she was scared. She'd told Maverick she couldn't take more of him never being around. Except she wasn't sure he'd actually heard her. They'd gotten engaged, and she'd barely seen him since. She didn't know what the solution was, but she'd hoped they could at least talk without her crying or him getting impatient and defensive or assuming this was all about something else.

Daisy-Mae was debating going home again. But if she did, it might mean they were breaking up, and she didn't want that. She wanted things to go back to the two of them having fun together again. Everything had gotten so heavy and full of business. It was just so…it was exhausting, and it brought out her worst insecurities. She hated feeling needy, and their current situation seemed to bring that out in her.

What if one of them was too flawed to make this work in the long term and in the real world? The world where everyone knew how amazing Maverick really was.

A few weeks ago, everything was marvelous and magical and wonderful. Now she felt like an eager schoolgirl with a crush, always at the ready for whenever Maverick had time for her. And because she'd said yes to an engagement so early in their relationship, it was as though he didn't have to try very hard any longer. He could set her aside and she'd be there. Happy and willing to please.

She knew it wasn't fair to feel this way, but she didn't know how she could make herself feel any different.

"You two are great together," Myles said, giving her a grin and a gentle nudge to pull her from her thoughts. He leaned against the barn wall beside her. "When we were teenagers, I thought he was going to fight me for you. Like, all the time." He laughed.

Daisy-Mae rolled her eyes. Any teenage girl with a self-esteem as low as hers who was proficient in flirting and wore tight clothes got a lot of attention.

"He always got a kick out of your pageant strategies. Especially when they worked."

Myles had spent years humoring her with appropriately timed grunts and nods. She never realized Maverick had been listening.

"He admired how you researched the judges ahead of time and asked around. You figured out the hot buttons and then avoided them. You were always muttering speeches under your breath. He thought it was adorable."

"I was just preparing," she said, feeling slightly defensive.

"He predicted you'd go somewhere big and great."

"Yeah, well. That didn't happen, did it?"

Myles gave her a strange look. "Aren't you in charge of some important stuff with the Dragons?"

"Yeah, but that's easy." It didn't feel real. Although the criticism Miranda got for Daisy-Mae's work and lengthy expense list did.

They were silent for a long moment.

"I got that job because I told some people off. I told them how to treat the players, and especially Maverick. And then he told them to give me a job. I haven't even been to college." What had they all been thinking?

Myles laughed. "I heard about that."

"When will I learn to shut up?" She'd ended up in this masquerade with Maverick because of her big mouth. She should have waited, pressed slowly into something that would have a chance to grow strong and lasting.

"Please don't ever learn that."

"But it's—"

"It's needed. Remember that time the protesters disrupted that pageant and you marched out there and told them their ideas were antiquated?"

She groaned. "That was awful." They'd shouted and blocked access to the event, and she'd taken them on without a thought. It could have gotten really nasty.

"How was it awful? You saved the pageant from being shut down. You informed them of all the ways these contests weren't anti-feminist." Myles spoke softly, tugging her hand away from her face. "For example, the bathing suit portion had been removed. The contests led to an increase in volunteerism. Fundraising was part of the effort, and scholarships were given to winners."

True, but if she started believing she was a crusader who opened her mouth and good things happened, then what?

For all the good, she'd also missed a lot of opportunities, too. She'd won thousands in scholarships but none of it had gone toward post-secondary tuition. She'd been stuck then and was stuck now. Stuck forever.

"What?" Myles asked.

She shook her head. "Nothing."

"Tell me."

"Myles..."

185

"We're still friends, aren't we?"

"Of course we're friends."

He waited a beat as though ensuring the validity of her words.

"So? What's bugging you?"

"Why didn't I ever go to college? I won all of those scholarships."

"There were always bigger needs," he said diplomatically.

That was true. He'd heard her complain many times about the pageant costs from wardrobe and travel to things out of her control such as car repairs and leaky roofs. The money was always gone before she could go anywhere or do something with her life.

Why had she even bothered with pageants?

"You know what?" Myles leaned back, studying her.

She glanced toward the barn. "You should go in and enjoy your party?"

"I think college would have ruined you."

Daisy-Mae blinked. "What?"

"All those businesses you started. I know it was hard. But you always stood by your customers even when it meant you had to pay out of pocket because of someone else's screw up. And you've always used your voice to make things better for those around you. I'm pretty sure business college would have molded you into someone you wouldn't like."

She waved off the absurdity of his claims. Of course she stepped up and did the right thing. That's what you did for your community, your customers.

"Someone always needs something," she said finally. It was the right thing to do, but it made it hard to get ahead.

"I love that about you. You step in when others won't or don't. It's what I like about Maverick, too. You're both great friends."

"Thanks." Myles hadn't always been one for giving her pep talks, but he was kind of rocking this one.

"And you're good together," he said, giving her another nudge.

"Yeah." They were. When they could eke out some time to actually *be* together.

Myles moved like he was going to head back to the party, but hesitated. "Promise me something?"

She scrunched her nose. "Do I have to?"

"He loves you. For real. I know it started as a thing to help him. But what he feels is real."

"Myles—"

"You need to open that big mouth of yours that you hate so much and fight for this one, Daisy-Mae. This is your one. Don't give him up."

She brushed her dress with shaking hands. "We're fine."

"He's my best friend, and he just walked in there like someone gutted him and you're standing out here alone. I might be dyslexic, but I'm not dumb."

She stood straight. "I didn't say you're—" She caught his teasing smile and relaxed. "Myles, I told him what I wanted, but he can't give it to me."

"Daisy-Mae, didn't you learn anything while dating me? You gotta tell us men things more than once."

187

CHAPTER 13

$\mathcal{H}$ is mom was practically buzzing around his house when Maverick got home from one of his whirlwind away games. She'd been delighted when he and Daisy-Mae got engaged, and he dreaded telling her they were fighting.

He dropped his duffle bag at the base of his recliner and fell into its cushions, exhausted. This whole being semi-famous thing wasn't for the old.

It didn't help that he hadn't slept much since the wedding, tossing and turning both nights while thinking about Daisy-Mae. He rubbed his eyes, fully expecting a thirty-year lecture from his mother, who had surely heard all about the fight through the grapevine. These kinds of things never stayed private in Sweetheart Creek—especially when you fought outside a wedding.

He opened his eyes before he inadvertently took a mid afternoon nap, ruining his chance of finally having a good night's sleep. There was a small table of plants in front of his living room windows that hadn't been there yesterday morning when he'd dragged himself to the airport before dawn. "Since when do I have plants?"

"They make it look like someone lives here," his mom replied, coming in from the kitchen.

"Someone lives here—me."

She gave a harrumph that made him smile, patting his cheek as she moved past him, bustling about, adjusting the plants. At some point in the home's history, the original living room windows had been replaced with two tall ones that stretched almost from the floor to the ceiling. When he sat on his recliner, he had a stupendous view of the rolling Texas hills out behind the house. And apparently, so too did the stray mama cat sitting on his windowsill, flicking her tail in irritation at having her peace disturbed.

"And since when does Kraken come in the house?"

"What an awful name."

"She has kittens in the barn. Penguin, Duck, Coyote, Panther, and Shark."

"Poor cats, named after NHL teams."

"I thought it was clever." He got up and traveled through the kitchen to open the back door off the laundry room. "Hey, Kraken. Time to take off." He left the door open and leaned through the doorway to check on the cat. She hadn't moved and was now licking her front paw as though she owned the place. Or more likely, waiting for her gourmet dinner. She was looking a lot healthier and less bony than she had two months ago, but he still didn't want her in the house. If she came in, he'd suddenly have six cats in here, and that was about three too many for him as a first-time cat owner. If you could even own a cat.

"I was wondering where you kept the food," his mother said, scooping the feline into her arms. Kraken purred, already knowing who was the boss even though he was the one that fed her.

"Her kittens are outside. She's an outside cat."

His mother cooed over Kraken, taking her into the kitchen and setting her on the counter.

"That's also where I feed her—outside." He swept the cat into his arms. "Off the counter." Kraken climbed up his shirt and launched off his shoulder like she was a slap shot sent from a possessed puck machine.

"Whoa." Maverick turned. The cat had landed on top of the old fridge, watching him. "I don't think I like feral felines in my house."

"She's not feral."

He picked up his phone and shot a text to Brant Wylder, Myles's brother, who was the local veterinarian and animal control officer. He had been meaning to ask if anyone was missing a cat. He figured two months late was better than never.

Had two months really gone by since he and Daisy-Mae found her?

Brant's reply was quick. The former owner hadn't owned a cat, and none matching Kraken's description had been reported as missing.

"What are you doing?" his mom asked, sending a pointed frown at Maverick's phone as he typed out a reply. She had begun telling him about his new plants that would surely die in a week and explaining how to avoid that.

"I'm asking Brant if he has a large, cat-eating dog."

"Maverick!"

He grinned and tucked his phone into his back pocket. "So tell me about these plants."

"I *was*." She huffed with impatience. "I hope you show Daisy-Mae more attention than you show me."

He sobered. His heart still stung from their fight, and he still couldn't solve the riddle of why they'd argued or when they'd have a chance to make up. Daisy-Mae was used to fame and attention. Yes, he was crazy busy. Yes, he couldn't always make their wedding plan appointments. But he loved her. And she loved him, right? They'd done okay earlier in their relationship moving their lives around. Shouldn't they be more okay than they were?

His mom reached into a large bag she'd parked on the counter. Her hands moved, but her eyes remained locked on him. He watched her watching him for a long beat.

"You always liked her," his mom said simply. "And I know she was Myles's girl for a long time. But I could always tell when she'd been hanging out with you boys. You were always brighter afterward." He gave her a look, and she waved a hand. "It's just one of those things mothers notice." She lowered her voice. "Myles is wonderful, but I always thought you and Daisy-Mae would be a better match. I'm glad you two found each other." She watched him again.

He sighed. He might as well dive into the conversation she wanted to have rather than let her wear him down. "We're fighting."

"About what?"

"She doesn't like fame."

His mom frowned. "You were both reaching for that sort of attention as teens—her with her crowns and you with your hockey. Looking to get noticed as something special. Are you sure it's the fame that's bothering her?"

"I *like* hockey. And my ability to mess up my reputation shows I don't care about being a celebrity."

"Or maybe it just gets you more attention." She gave him a smug smile.

"You think I sabotage myself?"

She shrugged, a bratty twinkle in her eyes.

She was teasing.

At least he was pretty sure she was.

He paused to consider the idea of self-sabotage, then discarded it.

"I think she doesn't like that I'm busy."

His mom made a sound of acknowledgment but nothing more as she unpacked containers of home-cooked meals into his fridge. She was clearly up to something. The two of them were close, but she didn't normally stock his fridge.

"Will this be a regular thing now that I live closer?" he asked, gesturing to the growing stack of containers.

"I bought you new bedding. I put it on your account at that new place in Riverbend."

"I don't have an account."

"I started one for you. Expect a bill in the mail at the end of the month."

"They let you do that?"

"Of course they did."

"You're dangerous."

"Just trying to make this place look as though you're not about to bolt back to the city." She cast a glance around, inspecting as she moved through the kitchen and into the living room. "You went a bit overboard clearing out your old life. Even I have a nicer couch than you do."

She winked at him playfully. She'd allowed him to give her the buttercream leather couch from his beach house as well as a few other items when he'd become fed up with his life being bigger than he was and had downsized it all.

Louis, when he'd heard Maverick was selling off just about everything, had sent him to the team psychologist in fear he was preparing to end his life.

"Why the stuff, Mom?" And why wasn't she hounding him about the fight? Getting into the nitty gritty of it and helping him figure out what was wrong with Daisy-Mae?

"You need to look settled."

"Why?" Maverick peeked into the living room again. There was a new painting he hadn't noticed earlier and a soft-looking blanket thrown over the end of the couch. Add in the plants, food, new linens.

The house didn't look so sparse any longer. It looked like a home. A home he really liked.

"Wait a second," he said. "Are you *nesting?*"

"Sweetie, a woman likes things to be cozy and welcoming. She needs to know you're not going to up and move out on her in the night."

"Daisy-Mae knows this is my sanctuary. I'm not going anywhere. I have cows." He gestured toward the kitchen where Kraken was still perched on top of the fridge. "And a cat."

"The right woman is your sanctuary." She turned on her heel and he followed her up the narrow staircase. His attention caught on a fern sitting on the windowsill on the landing where the stairs turned. If he wasn't careful, he'd knock the plant off its perch in the middle of the night. "This is nice." He picked it up, looking for a spot to relocate it so it didn't die on Night One.

"Don't move it. It'll get too much sun and die."

With a sigh, Maverick put it back down and mentally wished it luck.

"It likes the north-facing window here, and it'll do best with less light and more water. Not like the spider plant in your living room. They can survive almost anywhere, as well as being under the care of inattentive owners. I expect you to keep that one alive."

"Okay."

She grabbed the broom from the hall, and they went back downstairs. She put the broom away, then headed for the door. "In the fridge is bean salad, fried chicken, biscuits—"

"Mom, I'm in training. No carbs. No fats. At least not most of those." What was going on? She knew this.

"The food's not for you." She patted his flat belly and picked up her purse, which she'd dropped near the door on her way in.

"Hired hand?" Maverick asked.

"Daisy-Mae."

"Are you two having dinner here or something?"

"You need to invite her over, have a long conversation, and figure things out. You're being stupid. A woman needs to feel like..." She paused, her gaze growing unfocused before it snapped back to him. She sighed, suddenly looking tired. "Let her know you care. Let her know she's your choice at the end of every. Single. Day." She poked him in the stomach.

"She knows that."

"It's early days in your relationship. It's easy to feel insecure with you never being around."

"Daisy-Mae isn't—"

"She's human, just like the rest of us. You're a big famous man who could have any woman, and she might feel as though you're not choosing her any longer—like you got what you needed."

"I'm not like that."

"You need to be patient and fair to her. Your life just went completely insane, and she's never experienced anything like this. It's an adjustment." He opened his mouth to argue, and she added firmly, "This is different from pageants."

"So I'm supposed to say no to the money that will set us up for life?"

"What's the cost of saying yes?"

"What do you mean?"

"I don't know how you two find time to see each other." She gave him a pointed look that made him feel guilty, like he was choosing money over his fiancée.

Which he wasn't. He was choosing money *for* his fiancée. Daisy-Mae had never had it easy. He could give that to her. She could have a cushion that would give her the confidence to take risks with her career without worrying about what she'd eat if she got fired. Daisy-Mae was amazing, and he wanted to give her everything.

"She understands, Mom. She helped me get here. We'll be okay."

He felt like a liar. Things seemed to be getting worse rather than better right now. She understood, but there was a piece missing from his picture. Was it really as simple as her wanting more time with him and feeling insecure? For some reason he didn't want to believe that.

His mom opened the door, and he held it for her, his gaze catching on the rooster planted in his front yard. His heart ached for those lazy hours he'd carved out with Daisy-Mae not that long ago. Those hours that were so impossible to find these days. Was she just missing those moments as much as he was? Was it possible she needed them even more than he did?

"She's been pushing aside a lot in her life for you," his mom said.

"She's got boundaries."

"I know. But how many times has she let you down lately? Not been there when you need her?"

"Daisy-Mae isn't like that."

"And how many times have you not shown up for her lately?"

"That's—"

"Don't say different." She gave him one of those mom stares that made him straighten up and stop arguing. "Make sure you keep showing her how special she is to you."

"I tell her."

195

"Also try listening," she snapped. "I said *show* her. The poor woman probably feels abandoned." As she walked to her car, he was pretty sure he also heard her mutter something about stupidity and men, but he wasn't confident.

As he watched his mom's car pull out, he was left doing some mental math on how many times he'd let his fiancée down lately. It was a startling number nobody should be proud of.

DAISY-MAE HAD BARELY HEARD a peep out of Maverick over the past 48 hours until he'd shot her a text that afternoon, inviting her over. Curious as to where they stood since their fight, she stood in his living room on Monday night as the setting sun streaked it with rays of pastel colors.

She stopped in the middle of the room. "What happened?" The room had a totally different vibe to it. Less bachelor and more homey. "When did you get plants?"

Maverick had moved to the kitchen, and she heard the clinking of plates. She went to the doorway to see what he was up to.

"I thought we'd have supper. And talk about things."

"What kind of things?" she asked slowly.

It had been tense between them since Myles's wedding, and when he'd texted to ask her to come over, her first thought was that he was going to dump her. Now she was circling back to that fear.

She glanced at the food he was laying out, paused, then came closer. "What is this?" It looked suspiciously like food she loved. Food he couldn't eat while he was in training. "Are you sucking up?"

"Don't look so insulted."

"You left me at Myles's wedding."

"I didn't leave you there." His cheeks reddened. "You were the one who wasn't there when I arrived at the reception."

"After you asked me to the whole entire event, then bailed!" Her voice was shaking. "I ended up wearing the same color gown as the bridesmaids. I looked like I was trying to weasel my way into the family. And you weren't even there. Everybody thought we'd broken up and I was making a desperate grab for Myles."

Maverick stared at her. "Who said that?"

"Nobody. It's just... Never mind." She inhaled slowly, struggling to rein herself back in.

Maverick was still studying her, and she wanted to hide.

"I'm sorry," he said quietly, eyes cast downward. "I didn't think about what it might feel like to be at your ex's wedding. I know you two are still friends, and I knew a lot of friends and family would be there, so I didn't think about how it might feel to not have me there." He finally looked up, his eyes pained. "Especially on Valentine's Day. I'm sorry."

Her anger fizzled.

"Yeah." She leaned against the counter, feeling strangely defeated. "I should be stronger."

"You were with him a long time."

"Not that kind of stronger."

"The same dress thing?" He tried for a half smile to see if he could coax her out of her mood. His expression was so hopeful, so boyish, she had to laugh. She loved this man. She just wished it all was a little easier right now.

But maybe true love wasn't supposed to be simple and perfect. Maybe that was all some line that had been packaged and sold to her over the years, and she'd believed it because it sounded absolutely wonderful.

"What are you going to eat?" she asked, gesturing to the fried chicken, bean salad, and biscuits.

"It's cheat day. And beans are on Athena's Green list of foods."

"Yeah, but old farts like you don't get cheat days. And if you eat only the bean salad, you'll be an old fart in an all-new kind of way."

He gave her one of those grins that made her heart flip. She was such a sucker for him. And it looked like he was a sucker right back.

So, they weren't broken up. And it didn't look like they were heading there either. The lift of relief felt like a weighted blanket being tossed off of her. She hadn't even realized how much it had been weighing her down until it was gone.

They still had their issues, of course.

"Here." He started to dish food out for her. "How much do you want?"

She took over. "I can do it."

"Do you want to eat outside?"

"Why are you buttering me up?"

"Because I love you." He seemed nervous again.

"And?"

"We need to talk."

Daisy-Mae hated that phrase. So much.

"I know." She dropped the serving spoon into the container of bean salad a little too hard and stormed out the kitchen door with her plate, sending a gray cat scurrying away. Once outside, Daisy-Mae didn't know where she was supposed to go, and she slowed, waiting for Maverick.

He appeared a moment later and gestured toward the barn.

"I don't want to eat in the barn."

"There's a nice view just behind it." He had a fuzzy, cream-colored blanket slung over his arm. Wonderful for cozying under while watching a movie, but absolutely horrible for using as a picnic blanket. They'd surely ruin it. She thought about pointing out the error of his choice but decided that since he was trying, she needed to sit back and see where it took them.

Maverick led her to a small knoll that was dotted with wild strawberry plants. In a few months the hill would be speckled with the tiny red bombs of flavor. And right now they had a stupendous view of a field of early blooming bluebells.

Maverick spread out the blanket, and Daisy-Mae sat beside him. The view was gorgeous. Despite the setting sun, the day was still warm enough to sit without getting a chill.

"I'm sorry I've been so busy and have had to cancel on you so many times. I realized, like you said outside the Longhorn that day, that you're the one doing all the bending. And because you helped me get here, and had been in pageants, I sort of assumed you were well-versed in fame and attention and being busy."

"It's just been so overwhelming and sudden. I'm not *not* okay with it. At least on some levels," she said carefully.

"But?"

"It feels like I'm not a priority. It feels like you're always dropping me and assuming I'll be here waiting for you, no matter what. Like I'm a loyal dog who's happy with any drop of your attention." She could hear the hurt in her voice, and she hated herself for it.

"Daisy-Mae, you're not."

"I know!" She blinked back the sudden wetness in her eyes. "I know that."

"I've been working hard and saying yes to everything because I thought it was what you wanted me to do."

"But it's your career! Not mine. I'm not the boss of you."

"I thought you wanted this for us. It was the goal."

"To never be around each other? I'm not like my parents. I *waited*, Maverick. I waited for a really long time to find a love like ours. I didn't settle and I'm not about to start now."

"So enough is enough?" he asked, his concentration on his chicken.

She fought back tears, worried that he was angling toward her worst fear. But that would mean that everyone had been wrong about setting boundaries and telling him what she needed. And if you couldn't do those two things with the man you loved, then what good was their relationship?

"I wanted the world to see you the way I do," she said softly.

They had put their meals aside, frustration and hurt flowing off them both.

"But now everyone wants a piece of you, and there's nothing left for me."

Maverick shifted closer, carefully setting her hands in his. "You were the one who was always there for me. When nobody else was. You saw the truth. You saw me." He slowly leaned forward so he was in her line of sight. "I would quit hockey, Daisy-Mae. But I wouldn't quit you."

Tears came out of nowhere, spilling over in a torrent. "That's not true," she whispered. Hockey was his everything.

"It is true." He shifted so he was facing her, his body pressed against hers. "You're the most important thing to me. I got caught up in it all, but I want you to know this one very important thing."

He paused long enough that she said, "Okay."

"You say I quit, then I quit."

"Mav! I'd never!"

"You call the shots. You're my captain. You're my first team. Always and forever."

"MAVERICK, WILL YOU MARRY ME?"

Maverick's heart swelled at the earnestness of Daisy-Mae's request. She looked relaxed for the first time since she'd stepped into his house earlier. His absence had been weighing on her, and she'd had those fears his mom had suggested. He felt like a fool for not noticing it. He'd quickly become caught on that treadmill, thinking he was doing all of this for them and that it would be okay to get insanely busy so soon in their relationship—in *any* relationship. That they had already built a foundation strong enough that they wouldn't hit potholes that jarred the doors right off their vehicle.

She wasn't going to let him quit hockey, but she needed him to back off accepting so many deals. Most of that income would go to taxes anyway. So why was he busting himself to go get them? Because Louis thought it would elevate the team.

He almost shook his head at himself. The team was important, but not more important than his relationship.

"For real," she said. "Let's elope."

"But you hate the idea of eloping."

"I know."

"Your opinion has changed?"

"No, but if we have to wait for things to slow down in order to plan the wedding we want, it's going to take us *years*."

"Years? What if I retire or say no to more deals?" He'd signed a flurry of contracts over the past several weeks, afraid they'd get yanked back if he hesitated or public opinion turned again. He'd be consumed with extra work for quite a few months, but maybe he could spread some of it out a bit more to give himself and Daisy-Mae more time together.

"You're not retiring, Maverick Blades, number 53, captain of the San Antonio Dragons. Not yet, anyway. I can handle the time commitment problem, as long as I know you love me and that you'll start making me a priority and say no to things sometimes. Plus, saying no will make you more desirable because you'll be less available. You know what they say about playing hard to get?"

He laughed, pulling her into his arms. Their blanket had attracted most of the vegetation from the knoll already, making it a pretty nice barn blanket for the cats. But he didn't care. He'd buy another one. This moment was worth a lot more.

"You know, there's this old law on the books here in Texas," he said.

"Where we declare we're married in public three times and poof! We are?"

"Think it would hold up?"

"Maybe we could put a little more effort into our wedding than that."

"Okay." He brushed her cheek with his thumb. "How about we elope? We sneak off for two or three days?"

"You don't have that kind of time off during the season."

"I'll skip some practices. Can't skip a game, though."

"Yeah?" She was perking up. She liked this crazy plan.

"We'll leave right after a game and then arrive back just in time for another."

"Where would we go?"

He shrugged. "Where do you want to go?"

She smiled, dreaming.

"Then we'll have the summer to pull together plans for a real wedding before training camp. Maybe a fall wedding? September before the season officially starts?"

She nodded.

"We'll hire Cassandra to do most of the work because she knows us enough to figure out what we'd like. We'll have a Monday morning wedding planning date where we deal with decisions. We don't need to taste cakes or prance around town. We'll keep it simple."

She laughed. "Simple?"

"Are you going to be a Bridezilla?"

"I don't have time to be that. And as long as our wedding is closed to the press and any snooty types, I don't care if we even have tablecloths."

"We'll have that wedding. And it'll be good enough."

She frowned. "Good enough? You don't want it to be perfect?"

"As long as you're there, it'll be perfect."

He could see her considering his idea of streamlining their planning, getting strategic and letting the details go.

"And then once we're married," he said as she snuggled closer, "you can move in here. I can move into the apartment. We'll live together in two places instead of apart and in four."

She beamed at him. "And suddenly we'll have more time together!"

"That was why you wanted to elope, wasn't it?"

"Partly."

"It's a good plan."

She was nodding, thinking. Starting up that big sunshine mind-melting smile of hers. He realized it had been a few weeks since he'd seen it last, and he vowed he'd never get so caught up in something again that he forgot what was most important in his life—making Daisy-Mae smile.

"And date night," he said decisively. "We're going to have one of those every week."

"Where we'll choose invitation paper and fonts?" she teased.

"No, where I take you out and show you just how special you are to me. Even if I have to fly you out to Colorado or Calgary or wherever I have a game."

She opened her mouth to protest—probably over the cost or the fact that she had to work regular business hours and couldn't fangirl her way around the world after him.

"I'm telling Miranda that I'm stealing you away from time to time and that she's just going to have to accept it."

"You can't! I'll get fired!"

"They'd never fire you. Have you seen our ticket sales lately? The number of fans wearing our swag at games? Swag that you created, I might add. Miranda sees the impact of what you're doing."

"I still have to work certain hours."

"Going to our competitor's games is research," he said firmly.

She giggled at his seriousness. "I love you."

"And I love you. How does that sound for a plan?"

"It sounds—dare I say it—perfect."

EPILOGUE

*S*tanding on the beach, with the town of Indigo Bay and the bright rows of cottages behind them, Daisy-Mae couldn't stop smiling. She was getting married.

And she hadn't had to make a single decision thanks to Cassandra, who had recommended Zoe Ward-Wallace here at the Indigo Bay Cottages resort, to whip together a beach wedding. And it was perfect. Serene and private. Seagulls circling above as a warm breeze came down the sand to their spot near the water.

Daisy-Mae had brought Violet with her to be her witness. And because Myles was off on his honeymoon and Dak was up to his ears in his busy life, Maverick had grabbed the first teammate he could wrangle onto their late February flight. Leo, it turned out, was pretty good at keeping secrets. And so was Violet.

It was only recently, when Daisy-Mae had brought her head out of her own problems, that she realized Violet and Leo were on their way to taking over the world. And maybe not as two single people. That duo was full of secrets, and Daisy-Mae planned to find out what they were. But not until after her two-day honeymoon in the pink cottage just down the beach.

Maverick looked amazing in his tailored suit, and the breeze kept picking up her simple layered white sundress with the eyelet lace. Her hair was held up by seashell clips, and Maverick had found her some gorgeous, classic pearl jewelry. She felt like a relaxed beach bride but also someone pampered. Someone who had been chosen.

They stood under a rose-covered archway that filled the salty sea air with a gentle floral scent.

Maverick took her hands, grinning like crazy. She was pretty sure the world could end and he still wouldn't stop smiling.

I love you, she mouthed to him.

I love you too, he mouthed back.

The ceremony began and their vows went by in a flash.

"You may kiss the bride."

Maverick didn't hesitate, pulling her body against his, one hand to her lower back as he put his lips on hers. This was the beginning of the rest of her life. Of dreams coming true, of having a partner: someone who had her back and believed in her.

They would still be busy like crazy for the next several months. But she didn't mind as much now that she had the man she'd been crushing on, the man who gave her those slow, lingering gazes when he sought her out in the crowded arenas, locking eyes with her, then giving her a wink. She felt like she was the center of the world. His world.

Their leisurely kiss ended, and she expected to hear clapping from Leo and Violet. But when she turned, she saw that their white wooden chairs had been planted beside each other in the sand, and the two of them were locked in their own embrace.

"What is this?" Maverick asked.

"I think Cupid's found someone new."

"I do like that little cherub with wings." Maverick held her close, his body warm against hers. "And I'm sure glad he finally caught you."

"Oh Mav, he got me a very long time ago."

"I didn't realize you'd known Louis so long."

She laughed. "We should send him a thank you gift for pushing us together, because who knows how long it would have taken us on our own."

"Kiss me again."

"Yeah? Why should I do that?"

"We have a lot of lost time to make up for, Mrs. Blades."

HOCKEY SWEETHEARTS

Have you read them all?

The Cupcake Cottage

Peach Blossom Hollow

Sugar Cookie Country House

Chocolate Cherry Cabin

The Peppermint Lodge

The Gingerbread Cafe

There are more stories set in Sweetheart Creek, Texas in these two series:

The Cowboys of Sweetheart Creek, Texas

The Cowboy's Stolen Heart (Levi)

The Cowboy's Secret Wish (Myles)

The Cowboy's Second Chance (Ryan)

The Cowboy's Sweet Elopement (Brant)

The Cowboy's Surprise Return (Cole)

Indigo Bay

Sweet Matchmaker (Ginger and Logan)

Sweet Holiday Surprise (Cash & Alexa)

Sweet Forgiveness (Ashton & Zoe)

Sweet Troublemaker (Nick & Polly)

Sweet Joymaker (Maria & Clint)

MORE SMALL TOWN ROMANCES
BY JEAN ORAM...

Veils and Vows

The Promise (Book 0: Devon & Olivia)

The Surprise Wedding (Book 1: Devon & Olivia)

A Pinch of Commitment (Book 2: Ethan & Lily)

The Wedding Plan (Book 3: Luke & Emma)

Accidentally Married (Book 4: Burke & Jill)

The Marriage Pledge (Book 5: Moe & Amy)

Mail Order Soulmate (Book 6: Zach & Catherine)

Blueberry Springs

Whiskey and Gumdrops (Mandy & Frankie)

Rum and Raindrops (Jen & Rob)

Eggnog and Candy Canes (Katie & Nash)

Sweet Treats (3 short stories—Mandy, Amber, & Nicola)

Vodka and Chocolate Drops (Amber & Scott)

Tequila and Candy Drops (Nicola & Todd)

Champagne and Lemon Drops (Beth & Oz)

The Summer Sisters

Falling for the Movie Star

Falling for the Boss

Falling for the Single Dad

Falling for the Bodyguard

Falling for the Firefighter

ABOUT THE AUTHOR

 Jean Oram is a *New York Times* and *USA Today* bestselling romance author. Inspiration for her small town series came from her own upbringing on the Canadian prairies. Although, so far, none of her characters have grown up in an old schoolhouse or worked on a bee farm. Jean still lives on the prairie with her husband, two kids, and big shaggy dog where she can be found out playing in the snow or hiking.

Become an Official Fan:
www.facebook.com/groups/jeanoramfans
Twitter: www.twitter.com/jeanoram
Instagram: www.instagram.com/author_jeanoram
Facebook: www.facebook.com/JeanOramAuthor

Newsletter: www.jeanoram.com/signup
Website & blog: www.jeanoram.com

9 781989 359945